GRAVEYARD

A Glorious Collective Work

Copyright © 2016 by SEZ Publishing.

All rights reserved. No portion of this book may be reproduced, stored in a retrieval system, or transmitted by any form or any means electronically, photocopied, recorded, or any other except for brief quotations with citations in printed reviews, without prior permission by the author(s) and/or publisher.

ISBN # Hardcopy: 978-1533546470

ASIN# Electronic: B01KKJTJH0

In order of their apparition:

An Autumn Tale by Thomas A. Cerra

A Ghost to Kill by Lionel Ray Green

A Letter to Anna Bell by Jim Brega

Beyond the Sky by Katherine Scambler

The Big 4-0 by William Davis

Black Crows in a Cloud by Mathias Jansson

Cemetery Speed Dating by Michael Brodie

Churchyard of Destiny by Ray Jewell

The Clairvoyant by Erin Michaela Sweeney

Connection to the Other Side by Amanda Steel

The Dance by C. L. Norton

Dorothea's Diaries: Martian Requiem by Watson Davis

Dust by Kate Findley

Fryton by J. C. Michael

Graveyard Watch by Gweneth Leane

Heads by Rod Martinez

His Place of Rest by Bekki Pate

In Flooded Cemeteries throughout the State by Karla Linn Merrifield

Missing Since Tuesday by Ryan Howse

Morrigan by Suanne Schafer

Phone Call from the Mausoleum by Jill Hand

Pine Grove Cemetery by Skye Winters

Shock by R. G. Kaimal

St. Thomas by Paula A. Carr

Stuff by Larry Crist

Thou Shalt Not by Ann Martin

The Van Arsdale Secret by Mary Ann Ronconi

The Waif and The Void by Lana Bella

Witch by Kate Wiant

Edited by: Erin Machaela Sweeney, Kate Wilde
and Samantha Blackwell,

Cover photo: Kate Wilde

Illustrator: Elijah O'Mara-Mezzano

An Autumn Tale

by

Thomas A. Cerra

September began, feeling much the same as July and August, hot and humid without even the relief of a trickle of rain. There were however some noticeable changes, as the atmosphere rearranges its particulars. Mixed in among the bright green forests, which blanketed every hillside there appears the occasional tree whose leaves just cannot wait to change. Usually, this anxious Ent is a sugar maple or white ash, two types of trees that simply love to show off their true colors.

These are the doormen arriving early to usher in the season. To some this is exciting, to see the orange of fall. Others see only winter on the heels of a season that steals away the warmth and sun-blessed days they love: barbeques and fireworks, swimming pools and ocean views; such are the glories of summer. These doormen allow autumn to enter, and in doing so remind summer to take its glories and go.

As the month wanes and the October winds descend, the landscape and sky become a kaleidoscope of color. The musky scent of the season rides upon the breezes, an intoxicating fragrance that saturates the fall. However, for as brilliant and beautiful as these might be they are but a colorful distraction, concealing the thin grey wisps that drift amidst the gloaming. We see them as cobwebbed clouds twisting in the fading light, but in truth, they are so much more than what our eyes perceive.

    The ghostly host of autumn has such a subtle color we overlook its presence as it gathers in the shadows. The blazing hues fill our eyes and they ignore such forms disguised betwixt the garish delight that brightens every leaf. Gliding swiftly beyond the glow of the street light, this necromancer searches for disembodied souls, inviting them to join it as it races across the calendar to the destine day.

    We think, as people so often do, that we know all there is to know; our splendid conceit is almost laughable. There are, however, those who realize what stuff resides beyond our sight, but even they don't really know the truth. If they did, I believe they would be less accepting of the mysteries cloaked and conspiring within the umbra.

I have a friend who speaks to the dead and she believes that what they say is legitimate. Truth is what you perceive it to be and what you can prove of course. Nevertheless, a spirit will tell you any number of things usually from their point of view; unfortunately, that does not make it true. The story I am about to share, I cannot prove nor will I attempt, but this autumn tale most certainly changed my mind about what is and what might be.

As I walked a damp black street one night, beneath a grainy strand of light I caught a glimpse of something slithering in the dim. Startled I stepped back a stride, rubbed my palms into my eyes, and bent my neck to find a better point of view. Gazing into the swirling shroud, a puff of smoke, like a piece of cloud, rose up and rushed hastily away. I felt a chill, a bitter cold and smelled the stench of something old, musty as dead leaves after a November rain. Unsure of what I thought I saw, I chased this smoke for several blocks, until I found myself at the cemetery gates.

I stretched my chin above the balustrade, my eyes affixed on the gathering gray glowing beneath the rising of the moon. The last specks of sunset dripped away, blood red stains lingered eerily, and my heart began to pound in sonorous beats. A figure dressed in tattered threads, carrying a severed head, approached me through a fracture in the fog.

Aghast I compelled my legs to run, but instead they followed one by one the dank and crackling path of listing leaves. Face to face, I found myself chatting with this cloven skull, who said his name was Henri Laguille. Now I am just a normal man, not one to believe in fairy tales or creatures that hide beneath my bed. Nevertheless, here I am with this, conversing in a creeping mist with a head dangling from a specters grip.

Henri it seemed was quite insane, asking for Dr. Gabriel Beaurieux, insistent that they had spoken just seconds past. I assured him I was all that was there, except our friend, this ghastly ghoul who seems to be connected to the gloom.

"Nonsense!" he said, "he is the undead come to shake the witches from their chaste vows. He took me from a basket weaved, by an orphaned child left to feed on scraps swept from a café floor."

"Dr. Beaurieux, I heard him speak. He called my name after the guillotine had punished me for my wicked ways. I killed the child for a slice of meat, defiled her corpse without remorse, and then buried her beneath the painted trees. Her blood now drips from the tips of these autumn leaves. This being said, look about my friend, there are many things concealed in the charnel field."

My eyes careened about the lot, until they fell upon my family's plot where the souls of those I loved reside. A man in a grimy pinstriped suit with spats and rats about his feet lit a long and badly bent cigar. He leaned an elbow on the broken stone and then cocked a finger toward the unknown, a blank spot left un-carved on the family slab.

I knew this space was meant for me, but I wasn't leaving that easily. Not being dead I felt the choice was mine. Other spirits came to call. They fell like rain from every cloud, until there were no clouds left in the sky. Henri was smiling like a fool, his face aglow in the harvest moon as these phantoms began to swing and sway.

An orchestra crawled up from the mud with electric guitars and a man on drums that looked strangely like the Beatles Ringo Starr. His hair hung straight, his eyes but holes, his drums encrusted with rust and mold; still he never missed a beat. My feet too began to move; even the specter got in the groove, breaking out a twist on Don Pablo's crypt, a tomb in ruin yet still under lock and key.

Of all the things, I thought I'd never see.

"What day is this?" I heard me yell, as I watched the Broadway show from hell, prancing across the graveyard in a frenzied fit.

Henri responded with delight, "October 31st, a hallowed night, party time for those souls that just can't leave".

"But I'm not dead. Should I concede that this is where I ought to be?"

"Your day will come," a dark voice said, slow and deep "I'll arrive just when the time is ripe. Your type is oh so readily deceived."

Right then I felt my neck hairs curl and decided to vacate this swirl of madness, twirling out before my eyes. I backed away until my heels clicked, thinking 'this is what I get for sticking my nose where it don't belong.' Midnight rang from the church bell towers on old Main Street as the dark devoured every living thing left in its way.

I ran swiftly from the falling leaves, returning to the damp black streets where I first spied the sight of something strange. No time had passed, no moment spent. My curiosity I will long regret. However, there are still some questions left unsaid.

Did Henri ever find Dr. Beaurieux? Did he ever locate his arms, and legs; who or what is trapped within Don Pablo's tomb? Will the specter ever learn to dance? Shall the witches discover true romance and who was the man smoking the bent cigar? Sometimes, you know, a cigar is just a cigar.

In the morning, the world had turned to brown. The brightly colored leaves were gone and charcoal skies resided everywhere. The doormen had let something in with thinning hair and wrinkled skin and then abandon their posts like cowards often do. November winds blow cold and shrill, stripping every tree until the hillsides wear a beggar's coat at best.

The ghostly host arrives in splendor, vibrant as the fire and amber, but leaves a wretched semblance wandering in the cold. He is merely a drab, deceitful passerby with a wicked bit of twinkle in his eye. Neither sad nor in the least remorseful, his glorious days are but a fistful. What he came to do is what he leaves behind.

This story is my point of view, an autumn tale that might be true, but truth is not a gift one just receives. When a spirit tells you something else try to decide what you have seen and felt. And, if you notice a bit of cloud, perhaps you might want to think about those things that might exist amidst the gloom.

Remember, never lose your head or you might end up with the undead, dancing beneath the ashen light of a harvest moon.

A Ghost to Kill

by Lionel Ray Green

I never understood why people visited the gravesites of lost loved ones, but I do now. After all, I talked to my best friend Madison after she'd been dead for more than a month.

Madison and I are juniors at Pineview High School. Correction. Madison was a junior. On September 12, she disappeared. Seven days later her body was found in Laurel Lake. Accidental drowning, according to the local newspaper. Madison was reportedly intoxicated and fell into the water.

The principal and teachers acted appropriately sad at school. Madison's on-again off-again boyfriend Kevin seemed devastated as did my brother Mark, who was just a freshman but always had a huge crush on Madison.

The police chief called Madison's death a tragedy, but he was wrong. It was more than a tragedy. Much more. It was a murder, and I know who killed her.

Of course, nobody would believe me if I told them. I don't have any proof. In fact, I may never have any proof.

How do I know? Like I said, I talked to Madison, which happened to be Halloween night. That was no coincidence, by the way.

Here's how it happened. On the way to my friend Britt's costume party, I felt the urge to visit the cemetery at Maple Hill Baptist Church. I thought then it was just a random feeling, but now I'm not so sure.

I pulled into the empty church parking lot at 9 p.m. I felt self-conscious (or was it ridiculous?) because I was wearing my Halloween costume. I dressed up as Little Red Riding Hood if Red had skipped the trip to her grandmother's house and decided to attend a party packed with booze and boys. The skirt was too short, the cape too long.

The church only had one light in the parking lot, so it was dark. I used the light of my cell phone to navigate the markers and tombstones of the cemetery.

There it was. Madison's tombstone. Sweet, crazy Madison. The gray marble was too plain for her. She liked red. She liked gummy bears. She loved red gummy bears.

Madison had been my best friend since third grade: Madison and Stephanie. Stephanie and Madison. The dynamic duo. Now she's dead. Buried in a casket underneath the patch of ground where I'm standing.

At least, I thought she was.

I checked my phone. It was 9:12 p.m. Brittany's party started at 9, so I would be fashionably late. I reached in my purse and pulled out a bottle of Malibu Rum. I set it against Madison's tombstone.

"I forgot the pineapple juice," I told the tombstone.

That's when I heard it. A giggle. Not just any giggle. Her giggle.

I looked around, scared but not terrified. Goosebumps, yes. A desire to run for my life, no. I was completely alone in the cemetery.

"You forgot my red gummy bears, too."

My breath caught in my chest, and I fell to my knees. I couldn't see Madison, but I could sense her presence. A pinpoint of light hovered just above the bottle of Malibu Rum. Tears started dripping down my cheeks.

"Cry baby."

Where was her voice coming from? The light? Inside my head?

"Is it really you?"

"Yes, Stephanie. It really is."

I wept. I didn't realize how much I missed my friend until that moment. I had held myself together quite well since her death. Right now, I was a mess.

"It's okay, Stephanie."

After a couple of minutes, I composed myself and stood back up.

"Seriously? Little Red Riding Hood?"

I used my cape to wipe the wetness from my face.

"Do you have a better suggestion? I didn't have my best friend to advise me on what to wear."

"Actually, Little Red Riding Hood is the perfect costume, Steph, because I need your help to catch the Big Bad Wolf that killed me."

The pinpoint of light intensified for a split-second, and the bottle of Malibu Rum shattered.

For the next three hours, I listened. I didn't go to the Halloween party. I just spent the night talking to my best friend. At 12:19 a.m., Madison's light disappeared, and I left feeling better than I ever had since her death.

I had a mission. To catch her killer. I knew exactly who it was, but I'd have to wait a year before I could do anything.

You know how legends aren't real, except sometimes they are, like the one about Halloween. It really is the one night when the veil between the worlds of the living and the dead is thinnest.

Madison told me that I'd have to wait until next Halloween to spring our trap because of that veil. I didn't really believe her at first. I visited Madison's grave every night after that Halloween but couldn't draw her out again.

I would have to wait the whole year. It was difficult because I saw Madison's murderer almost every day. I had to pretend everything was okay. Even when her killer sympathetically patted my back and awkwardly offered to be a shoulder to lean on if I ever needed to talk.

I handled it all beautifully. I survived my junior year and spent the following summer break going over Madison's plan to catch her murderer. I knew it like the back of my hand, and when school started back in August, I slipped the first note of my senior year to her killer. It read: "Madison misses you."

Two weeks later I dropped the second note. "Did you love Madison?"

I watched Madison's murderer closely after secretly delivering the notes. I can say the killer was one cool customer.

On the last day of September, I left the third note. "Madison wants to talk to you."

Two weeks later I noticed Madison's murderer in the hallway at school, staring at a bulletin board and looking lost in deep thought, probably after reading my fourth note, "Madison wants to meet you".

"You okay?" I asked.

"Yeah. Just thinking about Madison. Can you believe it's been more than a year since she died?"

"I know. It seems like yesterday. Sometimes I pick up my phone and start texting her before I realize she's gone. What made you think about her today?"

For a second, I thought Madison's murderer was going to tell me about the notes. But the killer either had second thoughts or it could've been my imagination.

Three days before Halloween I slid the final note into the murderer's locker. "Madison needs to see you or she'll go to the police. Halloween night. 12:19 a.m. Her grave."

The trap was set.

On Halloween, I drove to the high school at 8 p.m. and left my car. I knew it would be safe to park there. I walked the fifteen minutes to Maple Hill Cemetery, slipping into the wooded area behind the graveyard where I settled in for the night. I wanted to get there early just in case Madison's murderer tried to scope out the grave in advance.

I'm glad I trusted my instincts because the killer arrived in a red pickup at 9 p.m., slowly driving into the parking lot and cutting off the lights. My eyes didn't need to adjust to the dark because the full moon illuminated the cemetery like a spotlight.

I saw the murderer exit the truck holding a bottle of what looked like whiskey in one hand. The killer walked into the cemetery and headed straight for Madison's grave. More than three hours early, the murderer stood in front of her tombstone, looking around nervously.

I wondered if Madison would reveal her light before the appointed time. Three hours is a long time to wait, but we waited. The killer sat down on the ground after fifteen minutes and sipped on the whiskey in silence. A couple of times I thought I heard the murderer softly call Madison's name.

Time passed quickly. I wanted to stretch several times, but I didn't dare make a sound.

Midnight. Less than twenty minutes until Madison confronted her killer.

Time slowed to a crawl then, the last twenty minutes feeling longer than the previous three hours.

I glanced at my phone. 12:19 a.m. Go time. That's when I heard the scream.

Until that moment, it never dawned on me that Madison might actually want to kill her murderer. Maybe because I never thought she could. I figured she simply wanted to face the killer and use guilt to coerce a confession or an explanation.

Then I remembered how she shattered that bottle of Malibu Rum, and I was scared.

If I'd thought Madison wanted to kill her murderer, I doubt I would've ever agreed to the plan. Madison was my best friend, but I couldn't be responsible for the death of someone I loved.

For you see, the killer was my brother Mark. A socially awkward teenager whose lifelong crush on Madison was more intense than anyone could've ever guessed. Unrequited love and all that.

On the night of my best friend's death, Mark had poured his heart out to Madison, who happened to be enjoying a buzz from too much Malibu Rum and pineapple juice. She'd had second thoughts about breaking up with her on-again off-again boyfriend Kevin after hearing he enjoyed a date with our friend Britt. So she turned to the rum to numb the pain.

If she would've been sober, Madison would've never met with Mark when he called and asked to meet by the lake. I imagined with Madison feeling hurt and vulnerable that some part of her wanted to feel desired. Mark would make her feel that. But when he begged her to give him a chance on that pier by the lake, she laughed. Or rather the rum made her laugh.

Probably heartbroken, embarrassed and angry, Mark pushed her away. She fell off the wooden pier, her head slamming onto a rock as her body sank into the black water.

Mark panicked and ran. Madison drowned. It happened just that fast.

Now Mark was the one drowning. In his own guilt. In his own blood. Madison could shatter more than bottles of Malibu Rum.

Tears burned my eyes as I slowly walked to the grave where Mark's body lie face down, blood pooling around his head, shining darkly in the moonlight. He'd fallen forward, cracking his skull against Madison's tombstone. It looked like Mark fell after drinking too much whiskey. Madison made it look like an accident.

"I'm sorry, Stephanie."

Madison's light winked out. I never even had the chance to respond.

I'm angry now. Madison killed my little brother, and I have to wait a year to see her again. At least I'll have time to do some research and work on a new plan.

I never understood why people visited the gravesites of lost loved ones, but I do now. After all, I have a ghost to kill.

My dearest Anna,

The fact that you've received this letter means that my worst fears have been realized, and that the happiness we have enjoyed together is gone forever. I only wish I could somehow apologize to those I've injured—you, most of all, my dearest—but I know that I can never see you again. I can only say this, truthfully and with my whole heart, while begging you to believe it: whatever pain my misdeeds have caused was unintentional and without malice. I know you will want to know *why* this has happened, but I cannot explain what I don't know myself. I must hold firm to the possibility that it was the result of an accident or a mistake. Indeed, I could not live with any other possibility. You know better than anyone, dear Anna, that I'm the gentlest of men. I flee confrontation and violence, am shy in public places, and avoid all argument and debate. Of what in my nature has made me the criminal I now believe myself to be, I know nothing!

Last night, in a dream state, I discovered where the man I had murdered was buried. I doubt you can appreciate the feeling of shock and terror that accompanied this revelation; you may imagine it was in some ways similar to what you're feeling now at receiving this news. I must admit I had almost forgotten about my victim, had finally begun to feel that I could go about my business without the burden of guilt and depression that, until recently, had colored my every waking hour with self-loathing and caused me to question my own sanity. I had almost managed to return to a normal life, had convinced myself—given the lack of any evidence to the contrary—that my murder fantasy was exactly that: a fantasy. I had even begun to imagine a future for the two of us....

But I can't think about that now. All those possibilities have vanished as suddenly and finally as a mirage in the desert!

I feel I can no longer keep my story from you, my dear Anna, even if it means that your thoughts of me, which once turned so tenderly to admiring my character, will henceforth be filled only with contempt and repulsion! But let me start at the beginning.

It all began about a year ago, at a time when I was experiencing unusually vivid dreams. I often awake from dreams with one foot still firmly planted in the imagined world, absolutely convinced that what I've just seen or experienced is real. Usually the incident is trivial; I forget these delusions within a few minutes, and the anxiety that has followed me into the waking world—over an imagined missed train, say, or my failure to acquire a mutton chop for dinner— quickly turns to vapor.

On a particular morning last year, however, I awoke with the firm conviction—nay, *knowledge*—that I had recovered the memory of having murdered someone. You can only imagine, my sweet, what affect this knowledge had on me; the more so as I realized that the dream was persistent: it did not dissipate in the gloomy June morning. I lay unmoving in my sweat-dampened sheets for several minutes, overwhelmed in turn by feelings of sadness, terror, and guilt. In desperation, hoping to force forgetfulness, I willed my mind to wander, distracting myself by examining the pattern of the roses on the heavy window draperies and the quilt mounded at the foot of the bed, the dancing light and shadow on the ceiling reflected through an open door from un-curtained windows in the next room, the spots on the carpet where an unknown substance was slowly bleaching the forest green threads the color of a tobacco stain. Everything made me think of violence: the crimson roses became (how could they not?) pools of blood; the flashing light was a reflection (in my imagination) from a brandished kitchen knife; the powdery spots were undoubtedly residue from some poisonous compound. After ten minutes, my recall of the nightmare had not faded. I dragged myself from bed, now enveloped in the noxious odor of panic, to start my morning ablutions, acting on the inspiration that a focus on quotidian activities might drive away all thoughts of the night before and the dream.

In spite of my discomfort, I felt fortunate that the nightmare hadn't included the details of the murder itself. I'm quite squeamish about such things, as you know, and can't bear to read in the newspapers and scandal sheets about even the most common violent crimes. In my dream I knew only that the murder had taken place, and that I, the perpetrator, had suppressed the memory of it until that morning. Who, where, how, when, why—these all remained a mystery. I had no further details.

Although I'd had persistent dreams before, they had never been as powerful or real as this one, and I'd always been able to come up with a way to prove them false. If I dreamed I'd lost my position, for example, I could easily disprove it by calling the office to announce that I'd be late that morning, quickly confirming through my superior's reaction that my mind had invented the whole thing. But how was I to assay the murder dream's pretense to reality? Here its lack of detail introduced an obstacle: I had never seen the face or body of my victim, nor heard him—I was sure for some reason that it was "him"—give voice to any speech or plea. He could be a stranger, someone I had never laid eyes on. How could I prove to myself that I hadn't murdered someone when it felt so real, and yet so many details of the imagined crime were missing? When the only evidence that it had taken place was a strong conviction resulting from a dream? It's said that suppressed memories can be uncovered through hypnosis; isn't it then likely that they could also emerge during the course of a night's sound sleep? Isn't it at least possible that these memories were of real events?

I managed to arrive at the office on time, if somewhat nervous and disheveled, and spent a busy morning in my dusty cubbyhole wrestling with customer account ledgers. By noon I'd begun to persuade myself, through sheer effort, that what I'd experienced was indeed born in my imagination and nurtured by my nervous disposition. I began to look at the other side of the question: after all, what evidence did I have of my guilt other than a dream?

But for the next several days I was unable to shake the feeling of dread and horror I felt every time I thought of my fateful vision. Gradually, I began to feel that my entire understanding of morality was threatened, and to wonder whether the mere fact that I'd had this dream, in and of itself, suggested an evil temperament. "Judge of your natural character," Emerson wrote, "by what you do in your dreams." Against my will, my mind began to wonder whether my "natural character" could include the potential for murder.

I resolved to visit my physician, Dr. Gutmann, to seek respite from the thoughts that obsessed me, either through a talking cure or, if that failed, a draught or powder that would at least allow me to sleep undisturbed. But when I told him my story he brushed my concerns aside.

"My dear sir," he told me, "You are interpreting your experience much too literally! Remember what Dr. Jung tells us: that dreams are symbolic in order that they *cannot* be understood, in order that the wish, which is the source of the dream, may remain unknown. I would be much more worried if you had dreamed that this mysterious figure was seeking to murder *you*; such a dream would be evidence of compensation for your own murderous urges. No, no," he concluded, "You must forget about this dream; it's not something that should concern you!"

I left Dr. Gutmann's office quite dissatisfied. I still hoped, in spite of his skepticism, that proving to myself that my experience was merely a symbolic manifestation of subconscious conflict would allow me to feel normal again, and I would be able to deal with this upsetting incident in a rational way.

As weeks passed, however, and a resolution continued to elude me, I began more and more to resist the nightly slow drift into sleep. I knew that, once my sub-conscious mind took control, there could be no way to avoid the possibility of dreaming, and I feared what would be revealed to me through that portal. In my tortured state, I thought it at least as likely that new revelations would damn me as save me. More than anything else, the answer to the question "Why?" tormented me. I couldn't accept Dr. Gutman's cavalier dismissal. Each night I paced from room to room, desperately returning to the clock on my mantle again and again, begging the morning to speed its arrival. I left the lights blazing and avoided the bedchamber, afraid that, in my exhaustion, I would be tempted to collapse onto the bed and there be overcome with sleep. But each morning I awoke to find myself splayed across a sofa or curled-up on the floor where I had fainted into a stupor at some point during the night. Blessedly, for whatever reason, I did not dream.

During the day there was no respite. I suffered from a constant biliousness in my stomach that no digestive could cure. Each morning I catalogued in the mirror the progressive change in my hair color from auburn to gray, the ever-more-prominent sagging under my eyes that darkened to the color of bruises. I saw an angry, miserable creature begin to emerge from my reflection, as if through a reverse metamorphosis: carefree moth to cowering grub.

Eventually, dear Anna, I felt I was left with little choice in my search for resolution: like historical and fictional monsters before me, I would plumb the darkest recesses of my soul, embracing the worst aspects of what I had come to see as my criminal personality. Acting on this impulse, I soon found myself immersed in the speculative study of circumstances under which I might, in fact, commit a murder.

Looking back upon that period, my complete absorption in this topic must have seemed like a form of madness to anyone who knows me. I sensed that danger and began to keep completely to myself but for the intercourse that business and the procurement of daily necessities required. My investigation, which took several weeks, would have been much easier had I felt comfortable contacting my solicitor for advice. My state of mind being what it was, I knew that would be unwise. How would I explain to him my new obsession with the study of murder, madness, manslaughter, punishment, and penance?

I won't tire you, Anna, dear, with the details of what I discovered. Suffice it to say that "derangement"—the one condition under which I could imagine myself committing such a horrific crime—is treated somewhat differently than other circumstances, as are intoxication, automatism, duress, consent of the victim, necessity, provocation, self-defense, and, simply, mistake. Such a rich landscape of excuse and extenuation! The law even considers crimes committed under these influences as "homicide," distinct from "murder," and defined as "the killing of one human being by another." How dry and unemotional! It sounds almost polite: "Forgive me, sir, but I feel I must kill you."

I seized upon this discovery as a drowning man would a piece of flotsam. If I had indeed killed someone, whether under derangement, necessity, or duress, who could morally accuse me? Perhaps it had been self-defense, against which no one could argue. It occurred to me that it was even possible the killing had been a heroic act, perhaps in the aid of some helpless creature. The fact that the incident remained unnoticed by the outside world, that I had not been visited by the police, and that my presumed victim remained unknown, were mysterious elements of the case; nevertheless my new understanding of the crime gave me respite from my fear of sleep. At last I could imagine an eventual reconciliation between my troubled mind and spirit.

And as more days passed without further dreaming, I did begin to put the experience behind me. I no longer avoided sleep, and awoke from each successive dreamless night a bit giddy, as though I had emerged triumphant from a harrowing experience. The daily confrontation with the monster in my mirror eased. As my conscience lightened, so did my spirits and demeanor. My countenance flushed with the roseate glow of rediscovered vigor. I began to feel that my fearful experience had made me a *better* man than before: less shy, more confident, an enthusiast for life and living!

It was at this point that I first met you, Anna, my dearest, my sweet! I'll never forget the day you knocked shyly on the open door of my tiny office and I looked up to see for the first time your beautiful face, your lovely eyes (hidden, though they were, behind your spectacles). I made some weak joke about "a kingdom by the sea" when you introduced yourself. You, charmingly, smiled at my poor attempt at humor. It's true your hair was unkempt, and your jumper had a dab of jam on it from your morning tea and toast—a dab that had fallen too high on your narrow chest for you to see it without looking in a mirror (a habit you obviously avoided). Still I was entranced. I heard nothing of your question about a customer account (Smith? Brown?) but stared, transfixed, imagining the transfer of that sweet dollop from your dress to my finger and thence to your pale, unadorned lips!

What a happy day, and how happy those that followed! I shall never forget our lovely sojourns in the fields outside the town. In my new, placid, love-intoxicated state, I even allowed myself to be persuaded to picnic among the headstones of the village cemetery, whence we'd followed the swells of wildflowers that had painted the hills with color. We sat and rested against the giant oak over the grave of Mr. G____, your head in my lap as I read you poetry, you playing the part of the maiden who "lived with no other thought than to love and be loved by me!" Whatever my fate, I want you to know, dearest Anna, that these last several months we've been together have been the most blissful I've ever known!

You may wonder why I've never spoken to you before of the events described on the pages you now hold in your hands; why—until now—I've never revealed to you, my closest friend, these terrible thoughts and dreams. Suffice it to say that I allowed myself to believe that I had put them all behind me, and hoped to share a life with you free of the burden of my history of crime. What must you think of me now? How you must despise me! I hope with all my soul that you will forget me, that you will soon find comfort in the companionship of an honorable man, for I can never see you again!

But I feel I cannot leave you without some sort of explanation, some narrative that will help you understand what has happened....

Last night I dreamed of the murder again, and this time the dream showed me where my victim is buried. Oh, how I wish it were an unfamiliar place! How I wish it were unrecognizable, an obscure spot in a foreign country to which I've never travelled, instead of the grassy hill behind my home!

I awoke early this morning in a state of panic. My dyspepsia had returned. I leapt out of bed and was sick several times in quick succession. I splashed cold water on my face, but when I raised my head to regard my own wretched image I didn't recognize the miserable being who stared back at me from the glass. Like Dorian Gray's portrait in Mr. Wilde's novel, my reflection told the tale of every transgression I'd ever committed. Every fear and agony I've experienced over the last few months came rushing back. Every rationalization and equivocation I had mastered was, in a moment, rendered ridiculous, and I am seized by a deep sense of hopelessness more complete than any I've known before!

What can I do? In my mind there is only one possibility: I must try to find my victim's body and thereby prove either that I'm a villain or that I've imagined everything. If I confirm the worst, I will have to flee; I feel I have no other choice. As much as I yearn to return to your arms, I fear, my sweet, that I would only ruin your name and find myself in prison if I stay. I couldn't bear that!

I've given this letter, which tells everything I know, to Dr. Gutmann, whom I trust implicitly. I've asked him to deliver it to you if I do not return to claim it from him by this evening. That will allow me several hours in which to search the location identified in my dream, to either discover the body of my victim or, if I'm unsuccessful, return to the good doctor retrieve this letter, and resume a normal life—secure in the knowledge that I've been misled by my visions; that I am, in short, not a criminal.

You cannot imagine how my heart breaks over the possibility that we will never see each other again! But I beg you, dearest Anna, not to try to follow me. I may leave the country, change my name, marry another.

And should you manage to find me again, who knows what I might do?

Beyond the Sky

by

Katherine Scambler

The sky showed no mercy,
sun glared at his grief.

Coffin pressed to ribs,
its pain a strange comfort.

Now the church was a box
of empty prayer.

Sweat beaded on the vicar's brow.
Cassock damp.

Light hung in dusty, garish stains
slanting through his haunted wife.

Head tilted,
she stared beyond the altar.

The graveyard
the skies,

Beyond the ghost of faith
hope.

The Big 4-0

by

William Davis

I can't remember exactly when it started. I think it was after I hit forty, maybe a little before. I do remember that a few months before my birthday I had caught myself on more than one occasion staring at the prepped graves of a cemetery that I passed daily on my way to and from work. Most people go through something when they hit the big 4-0; buy a sports car, have an affair, get a tattoo. Me? Turns out I was into funerals.

I'll be the first to admit that it was a bit uncomfortable in the beginning. Standing there amongst all the mourners who actually knew the person, I could feel their teary eyed stares boring holes in my fraudulent soul. Many would come to me afterwards and inquire who I was, how I knew Martin… or Beth… or Charlie, and I'd have no words. Usually I'd just walk away, leaving their already frail psyche shattered in perplexity. I remember this one, I think it was my sixth or seventh one; it was halfway through the graveside service when I realized I was the only white man there. Talk about awkward, you try explaining to a grieving husband why a strange white man was standing two rows back directly across from him.

See I think what set me off was the all-encompassing idea that we're going to die. I hear you all now; "Jerry you dumb ass we're all going to die," and yeah I get that, but before the *Grande Cuarenta*? Not so much. I think most men have that same problem. I think before we turn forty we are all thinking that we're going to live forever. We go to bed thinking it on our 39th year and 364th day, but when we wake up to 40 with death barreling into the bedroom straddling a freight train loaded with dynamite screaming; "WAKE UP JOHNNY IT'S TIME TO DIE", reality sinks in pretty fucking fast…Of course I've gotten myself sidetracked here. I was telling you about my obsession with funerals.

In my first three months I attended close to sixty funerals. That first month I went to one every day of the weekend; living in Chicago it afforded me plenty of opportunities. By the middle of the second month, I'd bumped up to two each day and had skipped work twice to attend mid-week services.

The third month, I received my first poor job performance review (attendance was mentioned, although there were other factors) and I was still able to squeeze in twenty burials, four cremations, and one internment at a mausoleum. You know what the funniest thing about that time was? My work missed me more than my wife.

I didn't mention I was married? "Was" being the proper tense; she left me month six. By then I'd already been out of work for a couple of weeks. My wife, Fran, didn't know that of course. I was an investment broker by trade and had built us a comfortable retirement that would've kept us afloat quite a while. The day I came home to the empty house and the simple note; "Jerry it's over, I'm at my sister's", I'd just been to three funerals.

The last had been a sunset service overlooking Lake Michigan. I don't know if it was the beauty of the silhouettes of the mourners carved into the backdrop of the setting sun or if watching over two hundred of my fellow human beings laid to rest finally took its toll, but either way I began to cry. It was the first time I'd ever cried at a funeral. I was so overwhelmed I literally took out my camera phone and snapped a few pictures -hind sight being what it is I really should've taken note of the two Marines in dress blues that were the brothers of the dearly departed before I succumbed to my emotions. It was because of those two that I stood re-reading Fran's note with one hand holding a cold rag against a warm bloody nose. That night I drank a bottle of Scotch and wacked off to the sunset funeral picture. Two days later I bought a shovel.

The first person I dug up was by no small coincidence the star of my first funeral after the big fortyganza. Her name was Mary Dorthea Smalls (June 27, 1947–February 20, 2012), she was a loving wife and caring mother. Mary smelled like sour old shoes that had been soaked in formaldehyde and then left out in the sun to bake away. Her loved ones had dressed her in what I can only assume was her favorite baby blue dress. They had strapped a double loop pearl necklace around her and left her hefty diamond wedding ring on her hand. It would be impossible to express exactly what was running through my head as I looked down on her. Peace, life, a squelching of the foreboding that had racked my brain ever since that stupid fucking birthday. Something like that and more, all of it mixed together into a sweet cocktail that swirled through the gut of my psyche. I didn't even realize I wasn't alone until the man hit me. Well tackled is probably a better description.

What happened after was/is a blur. I remember the sound of cold steel smacking into my head more than I remember the pain. Shouting; I remember shouting. "You fucking perve"…"We finally got your sick ass"…things like that. I remember my blood smelled an awful lot like a penny and then I don't remember anything.

It took two days for me to get in front of a judge. Apparently court doesn't convene too often on the weekends so when you're tackled, beaten, and subsequently arrested by one of Chicago's finest on Friday night you get to be guest of the city till Monday morning. Fran was there of course; my one phone call had gone out to family who would've immediately notified her. She was dressed in black, as if it was my funeral she was attending. Fran wearing that damn black dress confused me more than anything the lawyers and judge were saying.

Desecration of a grave, vandalism, and trespassing were the words that stuck in my head. My public defender patted me on the shoulder and assured me a $50,000 bond was the norm for such cases. I came close to inquire just how many grave desecration cases he'd handled, but then thought better of it. I paid my 10 percent down with a Cashier's check Fran had brought with her. She said nothing to me, her face said it all. I had become what she had always suspected, a creep, a pervert, and dredge of society. She was probably right.

In the end I pled down, that's what my lawyer called it "pleading down", to a single count of vandalism. The agreement was that I get six months of mandatory, state monitored, counseling. That was to run concurrent with my probation on the misdemeanor charge and I had to pay a $5,000 fine to the city and another $2,500 to the family of the late Mrs. Smalls for property damage.

Two nights later I dug up Frank Lyman; "beloved angel of God". They had dressed Frank in a brown pin stripe number complete with vest and bow tie. I thought it strange that they hadn't put his shoes on him.

It went that way for months. I'd make a stop at the local head shrink, then go dig up a few of my friends. I can't remember all the graves I visited in that time; I do remember that each and every one of them was special in their own way. By the time I'd finished my probation I'd dug up almost fifty people and was attending three funerals a day during the week and six on the weekends. The day my shrink told me I was fit to return to society I celebrated by attending a midnight funeral for some old guy who clearly wanted to inconvenience everyone he'd ever met by making them mourn in the night.

One day I stopped. I can't tell you what day – I can't even tell you what month. I know I kept going for years. I know my actions didn't go unnoticed; there were two write ups about me (both in the Sun), and the police would stop by and chat with me on those weekends where I got really busy. They were never able to prove anything, but it was always nice to visit with Chicago's finest. Then one day I was halfway down to meeting Ms. Margaret Chivers (teacher, warrior, poet) when I just laid my shovel down, climbed out, and walked away. I'm 49 now, tomorrow is my birthday. I've heard 50 isn't as bad as 40. My shrink (yes I still go every Tuesday and Thursday) turned the big half century a few months back and he said the only thing that happened to him was he started liking tomatoes; what a lucky guy. I hope it's something like that for me, but I doubt it. Last weekend, I found myself at Home Depot. You know the strangest thing was they were having a sale on shovels.

Black Crows in a Cloud

by

Mathias Jansson

The crows in the trees
Spread their wings
Fills the sky with a dark croaking cloud
A black flowing veil hides the sun
Shadows walking over the graveyard

From the dark moist grave
The caretaker stops digging
He looks up into the sky
Leaning his tired back on the shovel
Wiping the sweat from his forehead

Anxiously listen to the sound
The sinister sound of swarming crows
Feeling the chilling wind
The finger of death
Reaching out for him
He feels the hourglass inside his belly
The black sand spreading through his old body
Killing him slowly every day

Cemetery Speed Dating

by

Michael Brodie

At first, I honestly thought she was carrying a quiver. Which confused me, because, boy, did this ever seem like a weird place to be practicing archery.

"Hello there," she said. "Are you all right?"

Strangely, it wasn't until she spoke up that I even realized I was crying.

I didn't attend the funeral.

Just couldn't see the point. I mean, it's not like I cared about the ceremony. Instead, I gave it a few weeks until the headstone was done as well as installed and then visited by myself. Really didn't need the crowd. Figured if I was going to mourn, it would be better to do it in private.

Before arriving at Notre Dame des Neiges Cemetery, I wasn't exactly sure what to expect. Turns out the place is a lot bigger than I originally thought. It wound up being quite a hike to the gravesite. A ten, maybe fifteen-minute walk from where the bus dropped me off.

After I arrived at the section I was looking for and found the appropriate row, I stood off to the side for a moment. I needed to catch my breath and get my bearings before moving any closer.

This seemed like a nice enough spot, I supposed. It was, as I'm sure all the brochures advertised, serene. There were plenty of trees everywhere and the grounds looked well kept. Personally, the thing I was happiest about is that there weren't a lot of people wandering around. The whole cemetery was pretty quiet, even for a Friday afternoon.

When I finally approached the family plot, I was extra careful not to step too close. I hated the idea of standing on his actual grave, of standing on *him*. Even if there was six feet of dirt between us, it still felt somehow disrespectful. Since the whole point of this visit had been to come and pay my respects, then treading directly on the deceased seemed counter to the entire reason I was here.

Of course, if I was truly honest, this whole trip had a lot more to do with being able to *say* I'd come here than anything else.

And now I'd done it. I'd made my appearance, just as I'd promised, and the whole experience had been fine.

Fine, that is, right up until I saw the stone.

Until I saw his name etched there in a plain flat font. That's when everything came bubbling up out of nowhere.

All these feelings.

Where had they been on the day he died? I couldn't recall shedding a single tear after the phone call. Was I numb then? I didn't remember feeling that way. Maybe it was because we'd had so much warning. Long illnesses are like that.

But seeing this headstone right there in front of me, it suddenly made everything so real. So permanent. The ordeal was finally over and part of what I was feeling must have been relief. The waiting period had gone on for so very long.

How many times had I said goodbye? In person and by myself? Dozens? Hundreds? I think I'd managed to tell him everything I wanted him to hear. Probably several times over. There were no regrets left.

Still, at that moment by the gravesite, my emotions were certainly running hot. I was getting overcome with maybe the strongest sense of loss I'd ever felt.

"Hello there," said an approaching voice. "Are you all right?"

I blinked and everything got blurry.

My eyes had begun watering without me even realizing it. In fact, they were more than watering. When I reached up there were thick tears streaming down my face.

Jesus. I was crying. Actually crying. This was something I couldn't remember having done in years. And it's not like I was the type who bottled everything up. I just didn't cry a lot. Through my hazy vision I saw a female shape moving toward me. And it seemed as though she had something slung over her shoulder.

I wiped my face with the back of my sleeve then squinted in the direction the voice had come from.

After a moment, my eyesight cleared and I was finally able to see that what this woman was carrying wasn't a quiver at all. It was simply a large poster tube. I'd been momentarily fooled because of its shape and the way it hung down from her shoulder on a thick strap.

"Terribly sorry," she said, in what I now realized was a distinctly British accent. "Didn't mean to interrupt."

"Uh... It's fine."

"Listen, I know you don't know me, but I saw you there, looking vaguely miserable, and felt an urge to check on you. Which is probably a huge intrusion, I'm only just now realizing. So please feel free to tell me to bugger off."

"No, it's all right."

"Are you okay?"

"Yeah," I said. "At least, I will be. This, um, this little outpouring of emotion just came out of the blue. It's the first time I've been here. Didn't realize it would get to me like this. I'm kind of embarrassed."

"Don't be. Things of this nature can be very trying. If I may be so bold as to ask, the person who you lost was...?"

"My father."

"Oh dear. That's quite a big one."

"Well, it's not like his death was a surprise or anything. We'd all known it was coming for a while."

"Still. It's one of the biggest blows a person can face in this life. I'm Allison, by the way."

"Wiley," I said.

"Your name is Wiley? How interesting."

"Is it?"

"I don't think I've ever heard it before."

"It's short for William, actually. William Edward."

"So, like 'Will' plus the 'E' from Edward?"

"Exactly."

"Then why isn't it 'Willy?'"

"I don't know. The nickname happened when I was a still a little kid."

"I like it," Allison said. "It's very original."

"Thanks. Um, so... who are *you* out here visiting?"

"Me? Oh, no one in particular. Just working on my little project."

"Your project?" I said.

"I'm here doing some headstone rubbings."

"Headstone...? Is that really a thing?"

"Yes. It's my hobby. I take impressions of the images and words on select headstones."

"For real?"

Allison patted the tube under her arm and nodded. "Absolutely for real, yes. Would you like to see one?"

"Uh, sure. Why not?"

Allison peeled a plastic cap off the end of her poster tube and shook out something that looked like a thick roll of white fabric.

"This is my latest," she said. "Freshly produced not ten minutes ago."

She unfurled the outermost sheet from the roll and held it up.

"What do you think?"

"I'm... not sure."

The image was a reddish-brown reproduction of a child with wings, perhaps meant to represent an angel, but the style was incredibly simple, almost to the point of being cartoonish. Below the drawing was the name WHITTLE in block letters and a single year: 1859.

"What made you want to copy this one?" I asked.

"If it's all the same," Allison said, "I prefer to think of these pieces as having been *crafted*, rather than *copied*. I'm not a Xerox machine, after all."

"Oh. Sorry. I'm not familiar with the terminology. I hope I didn't offend you."

She smiled.

"Don't be daft, Wiley. It would take a fair bit more than that to offend me. Anyhow, I did this particular rubbing because... I liked the drawing. Nothing more. It spoke to me."

"Is that all it takes? For you to want to make one of these?"

"Usually. Sometimes I do one because I'm fascinated with the individual whose grave it is. Other times it's only because I find an interesting feature that I'd like to preserve."

"Do you have a lot of these?"

"A few dozen," she said. "Maybe as many as a hundred."

"Do you have a favorite?"

"Oh yes. A clear favorite. One I love above all the others and it never fails to delight me."

"Do tell."

"It's a plain stone, text only, and in huge lettering it states: HE LOVED BACON."

I felt a giggle coming on but tried to suppress it. I worried that if I let myself laugh it might unlock my other emotions and I'd start bawling again.

"And underneath HE LOVED BACON," Allison said, "In a much smaller font, it reads: Oh, and his wife and kids, too."

After that I couldn't help it. I burst out laughing. It took a moment to get myself fully under control.

I laughed good and hard, but thankfully it never shifted gears into me blubbering uncontrollably like I was worried it would.

"Bacon," I said. "That might as well have been my dad's epitaph, too."

"Oh. Not a healthy eater, then?"

"There's a reason why a man of sixty-two dies from—and this's how the doctor put it—natural causes."

"Sorry."

"It's all right. Good man, just a bit of a glutton."

"There's worse things for a parent to be," Allison said. "My mother, for instance, was very cold."

"You're right. That does sound worse."

"She's the whole reason I'm out here, actually."

"Out in Canada or out in a cemetery?"

"Both," she said. "But you wouldn't want to hear about any of that."

"Sure I would. I mean, if you wanted to tell me. I'm not trying to force you or anything."

Allison looked straight into my eyes.

"You would, wouldn't you? You'd actually like to know."

"Of course."

"All right then," she said. "I'll tell you. It started with my mother who, just as I mentioned, was a fairly cold woman. She made efforts to keep us sheltered, my sister and I. We were barely allowed outside as children and certainly never on our own. And even though a number of our relatives passed on over the years, she never once allowed us to attend a funeral. It wasn't until just a few months ago, when she herself died, that I finally set foot in a cemetery for the first time."

"Oh, she's gone? I'm sorry."

"Don't be. As I said, Mum and I weren't close."

"Then I'm sorry for that," I said.

"It's how she wanted it, so don't feel too badly for either of us. Anyway, there I was, my first time setting foot in a graveyard, and what I was immediately struck by was just how comfortable I felt."

"Comfortable? Really?"

"You have to understand, I'm a woman in her twenties whose entire knowledge of these places came from films, television, and novels. I'd half expected it to feel sinister or eerie. But of course it didn't. It was actually quite peaceful. After Mum's burial I found myself wandering the aisles of tombstones, staring, reading, just soaking in the atmosphere. It was like walking the halls of the most enthralling museum I'd ever been in. I got so engrossed I completely missed the post-funeral reception my sister put together for the family." Allison shrugged.

"After that, I suppose I was hooked. Cemeteries fascinate me now and these rubbings became a way of journaling my experiences. Mum left me a bit of money and I spent most of it on plane tickets and a used car. I've been tootling around North America on holiday, visiting different sites ever since."

"North America?" I said. "Why not Europe? I mean, you're from England, right? Unless I'm misreading your accent."

"London, yes. And I must confess, my main reason for being here is, well... this is so embarrassing, but I'm a bit celebrity obsessed. Because of my upbringing, all I've done since I was a child was watch things and read. So I've always found myself infatuated with movie stars and writers, and the majority of my favorites are on this side of the pond."

"So this whole trip of yours is really about visiting celebrity gravesites?"

"Not entirely. I'm also collecting unique artwork and anything I find whimsical."

"What qualifies as 'whimsical'?"

"I'm glad you asked that, Wiley."

Allison began unfurling another sheet from her roll.

"This piece is actually the main reason I came to this particular cemetery. Montreal, it turns out, is home to one of the most famous headstones in the world. And trust me, I'm not winding you up when I tell you that this one is an absolute must-have for any collector."

She held the sheet up. This rubbing, done in a dark purple hue, was composed of seven lines of text arranged in the style of a poem or maybe an ode.

"Give this a quick read," Allison said. "Then tell me if you can see why I think it's so bloody brilliant."

JOHN:

FREE YOUR BODY AND SOUL.

UNFOLD YOUR POWERFUL WINGS.

CLIMB UP THE HIGHEST MOUNTAINS.

KICK YOUR FEET UP IN THE AIR.

YOU MAY NOW LIVE FOREVER.

OR RETURN TO THIS EARTH.

UNLESS YOU FEEL GOOD WHERE YOU ARE!

After I finished reading the lines, I turned to Allison, confused. This wasn't anything special.

"Don't you see it?" she said.

"All I see is a bunch of very mediocre sentimental drivel."

"Look again. And this time pay particular attention to the letter placement. I guarantee it will change your opinion of what the deceased's friends actually thought of him."

On my second pass I caught the joke right away. Reading the first letter of every line straight down revealed a deceptively simple phrase hidden in plain sight.

"Oh man," I said. "I cannot believe someone had that inscribed on a real tombstone."

"And yet they did. You can see the original for yourself, it's just a few rows away from your father."

"Aren't there usually laws against this?"

"Against being clever? None that I know of."

"What a world," I said. "And this is the stuff you're traveling around doing rubbings of?"

"As well as the celebrity ones."

"Captured anyone I'd have heard of?"

"Depends. Are you familiar with Bruce Lee?"

"Of course."

"He was my first on this side of the world. Followed by Jimi Hendrix. Oh, and Chris Penn. They're all in Seattle, where my flight landed, and it's also where I bought my car."

"Um... the other two I understand wanting. They're legends. But... *Chris Penn?*"

"I liked his early career, before he got really fat."

"You must be quite a cinephile."

"Guilty," Allison said. "But I like people who are famous for other reasons, too. For instance, after Seattle, I made my way north to Port Coquitlam where I visited Terry Fox. And after that I headed east to Owen Hart in Calgary, then Marshall McLuhan in Toronto, and just a few miles up the road I popped in on Corey Haim in Vaughn."

"Remind me," I said. "Who's Corey Haim again?"

"Famously one of The Two Coreys. You don't know him? He was one of the kids in *The Lost Boys*."

"Oh right."

"He has one of my favorite gravestones. It's all very dignified and appropriately mournful... until you get to the corner where they engraved *Haimster*, which I suppose was his nickname."

"Ouch. That is pretty awful."

"Not all gravestones are outright masterpieces," Allison said. "And speaking of which... I still haven't taken a proper look at yours. May I?"

"Uh, okay."

Allison crouched down to examine my father's stone more closely.

"Oh dear," she said.

"What's wrong?"

"Well, there's really nothing here. Just the name and dates. No 'beloved' this or 'dearly missed' that. Can I ask...? Were there any problems at the end? Was someone cross with him when he died?"

"What? No. Why would—?"

"But it's so *plain*," Allison said. "If you really cared then wouldn't you have—?"

"What are you saying? Of *course* we cared. We... we all really loved him."

"Oh wait," she said. "I'm being stupid. I hadn't noticed before. But his name was Edward. Same as you. Your middle name. Which means... well, forget about this cold piece of stone. We've found the real monument, then, haven't we?" She stood and placed a hand on my arm.

"It's you, Wiley. You're the monument. You share his name. Which means... well, it means you never need to miss him because you'll always carry that small piece around with you, forever."

I felt my throat tightening.

"But... but I do miss him. He..."

My eyes began to sting as they welled up with fresh tears.

"Excuse me... I..."

It was getting hard to speak.

"Oh no," Allison said. "I've gone and upset you again. I'm so sorry, Wiley."

In between gentle sobs, I managed a few words.

"It's... it's okay."

"No, no. This is all my fault. Damn. I wish I could take back what I said. Or think of something I could do to make up for it."

Allison took my hand very gently in hers and squeezed it reassuringly.

"Fancy a fuck?" she said.

"I... huh?"

"A fuck. Would that make you feel better?"

"I... Wait, *what?* For real?"

Allison nodded.

From our spot behind some dense shrubbery, I could hear a few people passing by and making quiet conversation on their way deeper into the cemetery.

I was lying on two blank sheets of the material from Allison's poster tube. She'd unrolled them onto the ground before undoing my pants and mounting me.

After we were done, she lay next to me, her cheek against my chest, breathing slowly, one of her hands tenderly fondling my still-wet cock.

"On Sunday I'll be heading for Baddeck."

"Sorry, what?" I said.

"You asked me a minute ago where I was heading next. I'm off to a village in Nova Scotia called Baddeck. Alexander Graham Bell is buried there. Unfortunately, his remains are on a private estate. May have to trespass if I want to snag a rubbing. And I haven't done any legwork yet. Hopefully it won't be impossible."

"Have you ever been arrested doing this?"

"I've had a few warnings, nothing more. Anyway, on Sunday I'm off to Nova Scotia and from there it's on to P.E.I. and Lucy Maud Montgomery. But tomorrow, before I leave town, I'll be back in this neighborhood."

"Back here?" I said.

"No. Just down the road, at Mount Royal Cemetery. Anna Leonowens is buried there."

"And she is...?"

"She's Anna. *The* Anna. The governess from *The King and I.*"

"That's a real person? And she's buried in Montreal?"

"Yes to both," Allison said.

"I had no idea. So then, um, since you'll be over there tomorrow, would you mind if I—?"

"Let me stop you right there, darling. This was a one off."

"A what?"

"A one-time thing. Those are the rules."

"Rules? Why are there rules?"

"Damn. I misspoke. Let's just pretend I never said anything, okay?"

"Allison, what are you talking about? Why are there rules?"

"Oh dear. I've stepped in it, haven't I? Promise you won't get mad?"

"Why would I get mad?"

"Because... I did it on purpose."

"Did what?"

"Those things I said before. About your father. I triggered you intentionally. In the hopes you'd get upset."

"What? Why?"

"I want you to know," Allison said, "That I didn't start out doing this on purpose. I really was just out here on holiday, innocently making headstone rubbings and taking a tour of the country. But once I discovered it, it kind of altered the course of my trip."

"Discovered what?"

"Grief sex," Allison said. "I didn't know until I stumbled onto it, but grievers make for amazing lovers. And, sure, you have to stop every once in a while if they start a crying jag or pound their fists against your chest because of the unfairness of it all. But there's so much *passion*. I think it has something to do with the whole 'I just want to feel alive' thing that follows a confrontation with death."

Allison paused, then turned her eyes up to mine before continuing.

"The truth is," she said, "I'm working on *two* collections now. The first is the one I've already mentioned, while the other, well, the other involves *you*, and people in your situation."

She paused again and then said: "I hope you don't hate me."

"What? No."

"Even though I deceived you?"

"It's definitely a little weird, but I certainly don't hate you. Really, I'm still very happy we met."

"God, Wiley, you're just so sweet." She hugged me tight and then said, "Listen, if it isn't too much to ask, may I make one final request of you?"

After using copious amounts of masking tape to secure the sheet, Allison took a cake of rubbing wax and began drawing it across the surface of my father's headstone. She made her way in from the outer edges, diligently working at it until the image was completely filled in.

"Some people use butcher paper," she said, "But I prefer this non-fusible interfacing."

"What's that?"

"A kind of fabric. It's not important. Just shop talk."

"I don't mind," I said.

"I think I'm done." She stood up to admire her handiwork.

"Looks nice."

"It does, doesn't it? Forget what I said earlier. It's a fine-looking stone. Plenty of character."

"Thanks."

"I feel so good right now," Allison said. "And I'm really looking forward to the next leg of my trip."

"Yeah?"

"After I visit Bell and Montgomery, I've decided to circle back down south and circuitously wind my way over to Baltimore."

"What's in Baltimore?"

"This might sound like a terrible cliché, especially given the dark aspect of my little hobby, but I'm going to finish up my trip with Edgar Alan Poe's headstone."

"Actually, that seems pretty apt."

"I know, right?" Allison said, "Although... if I have any energy left by then, I may continue on for one last leg and swing up to Lake Forest in Illinois."

"What's there?"

"Another writer's grave. One who has a lot more personal meaning to me than old Edgar Alan."

"Who?"

"John Hughes," she said.

"*The Breakfast Club* guy?"

"Yes. And while his work may not be quite as timeless as Poe's, Poe never wrote a line anywhere near as eloquent as 'You break his heart, I break your face.'"

"What's that from?"

"You don't know it? Let me try another quote from the same film. Ahem. 'This is what my girlfriend would look like without skin.'"

"Oh, that is really familiar."

"It's from *Some Kind of Wonderful*. Which is probably my all-time favorite movie. I can recite every line from it verbatim. Feel free to test me."

"You're so adorable," I said.

"Oh, don't be fooled," Allison said. "I may seem cute as a button right now, but I'm really not."

"What are you talking about?"

"Just being realistic. You see, out in the real world, I'm a six at best. On a scale of one to ten. A bit plain for most people's tastes."

"You're crazy."

"No, not at all. I'm a six, maybe a six and a half on a really good day. But here's the thing: while I may be a real world six, I also happen to be a graveyard eight. Maybe even a nine."

"Seriously, you're talking crazy."

"The fact is, Wiley, you're wearing grief goggles. On top of which, there's really no competition out here. And if there's one thing I know about myself, it's that I do fantastically well when there's little to no competition."

"Oh, stop it."

"There's this old Dorothy Parker quote, one I've adapted for my own uses... It goes something like this: 'Men seldom make passes at girls lying in caskets.'"

I think my mouth may have dropped open.

"Oh, you did not just say that."

"Oh, but I did," she said, grinning.

"What would you call this, anyway, this secondary hobby of yours? I mean, if you had to give it a name. Would it be something like... cemetery speed dating?"

"No, darling. Let's be realistic. It's much more along the lines of... cemetery sport fucking."

"You are really something else."

"I try my best not to disappoint."

Allison knelt back down and began tearing the strips of masking tape off my father's headstone.

"Listen," I said. "May I ask one favor?"

"Sure. What is it?"

"Reconsider. Let me join you tomorrow up the road at... at what's her name's grave site."

"Anna Leonowens. But no, I'm sorry, Wiley, I have to refuse. I'm just not all that interested in men who are past the peak of their grief."

"Think about it, okay? I'd really like to see you again before you leave town."

Allison tore off the last of the tape and began rolling up the finished rubbing.

"I promise," I said, "I'll still be sad tomorrow."

Allison looked back at me over her shoulder and smiled.

"You better be."

Churchyard of Destiny

by

Ray Jewell

Roger had been watching the distinguished looking man visiting the Carter gravesite for nearly two years, and in all the years that he'd been caretaker of this churchyard, he was the only one. A pleasant enough gentleman, he thought, having chatted with him from time to time about bits of this and that.

A doctor, he'd been told, although Roger suspected the gentleman might have been a remote relative of some kind. Later, he discovered he was just someone who had taken an interest in the genealogy of the Carter woman. But no matter, he left a bouquet of roses on each visit, nodded at him and quietly left. When he did, the mystery of his visit left with him.

The doctor of course, had continued visiting the gravesite, but since the laboratory explosion a few days ago at the research center, things had been getting a bit strange around the churchyard.

Roger remembered back when the doctor was in a particularly talkative mood. He enjoyed Roger's company, probably because he was such a good listener.

He'd patiently listened to the doctor relate stories of scientific achievements and theories, although he couldn't grasp any of the concepts being described. As a physicist, one of his favorite topics was time travel, his firm belief that science had already provided the groundwork for its use. Of course, this interest was related to the subject buried before them.

The inscription on her headstone was simple, but eloquent:

Here lies the mortal remains of the Heart of Melrose
Catherine Rose Carter, MD
21 November 1865–17 December 1927

Dr. Ed had told him that he'd found her because of some necessary research he'd done at the old city library of Melrose. Old in the sense that it'd accumulated a couple hundred years of diaries, newspaper clippings, photographs and old family bibles since it had been built in the early 1800s.

On the wall of the reading room at the library were scores of antique photographs, depicting portraits of city notables and scenes of life in the area as it was over a century ago. One picture in particular managed to catch the doctor's interest, and in time became his obsession.

The doctor described a portraiture of a middle-aged woman that looked out over the room, her face smooth and comely in a classic sense. Her eyes had looked directly into the camera lens, giving the photographed subject the appearance of looking directly at the viewer. Full, curved lips, turned up gently at the corners suggested a curious sense of humor, and to the doctor, a sensuous nature that he found irresistible. He had fallen in love.

Researching that photograph revealed that the woman was a medical doctor, and had practiced in the town during the late 1800's. She passed away at the turn of the century. A spinster, she'd devoted her entire life to the health and well-being of the inhabitants of Melrose.

Further research led him to this small churchyard near the

edge of the city, containing considerable historical value for the region, and a small graveyard. Beneath an immense oak tree, he'd found her; or at least her last resting place. The grave was a bit isolated from the others, as though she'd earned some special status from her contemporaries.

Although Roger had a hard time believing it, Dr. Ed described himself as a painfully shy person all his life, and while this trait served him well in his academic and professional life, it left him lacking in social skills. His interests consisted of the realm of scientific study and research, and little else. Finding a companion who shared these interests, at least to the degree that he did, was nearly impossible, particularly with the opposite sex.

The doctor would often let his imagination soar, and enter a world of 'What if…?' on some visits, entertaining Roger with stories of going back in time to meet this woman, obviously a person of science, to woo and marry. Shaking his head, he'd expound on the impossible energy requirements to perform such a 'time shift', and of the danger involved even to attempt to generate power of that magnitude.

Roger knew that wasn't possible; he might be a bit slow, but he wasn't that foolish. Whenever the doctor finished with these impossible tales, they'd share a laugh or two and get on with their day; the doctor off to do whatever it was he did, and Roger to his grounds keeping duties.

But still, the doctor was a kind man; one could tell by the roses he brought to the grave each time he visited, and the occasional package of Roger's favorite pipe tobacco he often brought for the caretaker. As the weeks and months rolled by, Roger and the doctor developed an unlikely, but close relationship.

Now Roger's mind was beginning to play tricks on him, he thought. Memories of some events seemed to be fading, and he was worried that they'd soon be lost altogether. Folks already thought that he was kind of slow, but now something was happening that he couldn't understand.

If Dr. Ed was there, he'd know what to do, he thought, but

he'd not appeared at the gravesite since the big explosion at the laboratories.

The day before he'd gone to the churchyard to tidy up the area, and he spied a young lady on one knee before the Carter plot, placing a bouquet of roses before it. Oddly, she seemed familiar, but he couldn't recall where he might have seen her before. As she rose to leave, Roger noticed a disturbance in the soil next to the headstone, as if it had been scraped clean to accept another resident.

Burials were no longer allowed in this graveyard since the late 1930's, once the state granted it special historical status before the outbreak of World War II. And, if there were any exceptions to be made, he'd have been one of the first to be notified, he thought.

While some memories seemed to be fading, others seemed to be firmly slipping into his mind, becoming more familiar as time marched on. If he didn't know better, he'd have thought that his entire life was being re-written.

Now it'd been several days since the huge explosion at the research center, and it appeared that there were no victims. Cleanup and repair was underway, and the townsfolk were expressing relief at the restoration of the areas primary employer.

Roger however, was still trying to deal with the conflicting memories rolling through his mind. For a few days he felt that he was possessed by someone else, or that he was actually experiencing the thoughts of two different people. If only, he thought, the doctor was there.

That morning he arose as usual, discovering that several things around his home had been rearranged, and there were items that he didn't remember having previously, replacing more familiar items. Most surprisingly, he saw a couple of photographs perched on an unfamiliar coffee table, with images of him in the embrace of a beautiful young woman, flanked by two young ladies, obviously twins.

Suddenly the recollection of the young lady at the gravesite the previous day struck him. She was familiar, one of the twins in the photograph. He'd rambled through the house, noting anomalies from his earlier memory of his home. Even the smells were different; more feminine, he decided, and the rooms appeared to be much neater than was his custom to maintain.

He was frightened, afraid that his mind was finally giving way to madness. More thoughts were crowding into his head now, names; memories; subtle impressions of places visited and deeds performed. The more he fought these thoughts back, the stronger they seemed to become.

Carrie; the name came to him accompanied by a strong feeling of warmth, comfort and yes, even love. The longer he stared at the family portrait, the more familiar it became, and memories crept into his mind unbidden.

He left the house quickly towards the churchyard, hoping that his daily work routine would bring him back to normalcy. It was all in vain however, as waves of new memories followed him to the small graveyard.

There, he was confronted by another small shock; the

Carter gravesite was no longer the same. Where once stood a small, lonely headstone, another larger one stood in its stead. Cautiously approaching the site, he carefully took note of the fresh addition to the area. Perhaps fresh wasn't the best description, as the stone appeared quite weathered, and the ground surrounding it now seemed completely undisturbed. In the shade of the huge oak, he slowly made out the inscription on the large stone.

Henderson Family

Beloved Husband and Father	Beloved Wife and Mother
Edward Paul	Catherine Rose (Carter)
Scientist	Physician
circa 1861–08/28/1920	11/21/1865–12/17/1927

As he stood before the headstone in shock, he was startled when a small, warm hand slipped into his. Glancing over to see who it was, he saw Addie, his daughter, one of the twins standing beside him.

Addie? Daughter? Recollections were rushing into his

mind, and images of Maddie, his other daughter quickly flashed across his mind. Carrie, his wife had displayed her wonderful sense of humor in naming their lovely daughters Adeline and Madeline, his beautiful twin daughters; how could he have forgotten?

It appeared that the irresistible force flooding his mind was building him a family, banishing his bachelorhood forever. He was giving into this force, only curiously wondering what was becoming of his bland, sterile past.

He was now beginning to remember some additional things. His mother-in-law's married name was Henderson, and she resided in a retirement community some 600 miles from there. So many things to assimilate, he wondered.

His daughter released his hand, moving to the gravesite to rearrange the bouquet of roses, which had scattered because of the wind sweeping across the yard.

Flush with fresh memories, there was one other thing to check out, Roger thought, while his old memories still lingered, and returned to his vehicle. Driving to the library, he wanted to check out the portrait of Dr. Carter once again, just to satisfy his newfound curiosity regarding events happening with him.

Stepping into the 'Hall of Portraits' as it was called, he searched the wall for her photograph. Eventually he found it, but what he discovered was not what he remembered. But then, these older memories were fading still, replaced by these newer, more intense ones.

The photograph before him contained images of both Dr. Ed and in his arms, a very happy Dr. Carter; or rather, Dr. Henderson. Looking at the photograph more closely, Roger could just make out the faint outlines of writing at the bottom, bleached orange a bit by age and sunlight, but still legible.

"To my best friend Roger; if you can dream it, you can accomplish it. Believe. ~ Ed."

As he absorbed the implication of that message from the past, he began to choke up a bit. It was clear to him now that he'd not see his friend again. In his stead, Roger now had a family, and a lifetime of companionship that he'd never have conceived of before.

The sound of someone familiar clearing their throat behind him broke into his thoughts, and he turned to see his wife, Carrie. Even more beautiful than the picture he viewed in his home that morning, he lost himself in her gaze, lovely deep blue eyes reflecting his love for her.

"I could never understand your fascination with my grandparents, Roger, but I'm eternally grateful that I chose you to be my companion in this life." She said. Embracing him, she kissed his cheeks tenderly.

He read the small tag beneath the picture, describing how the two scientists had struggled during the Influenza Pandemic of 1918–1920 to save the affected citizens of Melrose, and between the radical procedures created by Dr. Edward Henderson, and the medical expertise of his wife, Catherine, Melrose had survived the calamity relatively untouched. The only notable casualty was Edward himself, who ultimately succumbed to the disease in 1920. They were survived by a daughter, Eunice in Chicago

In the embrace of his beloved wife, Roger silently thanked Dr. Ed for his gift, and hoped that the doctor's dream was all he'd thought it would be.

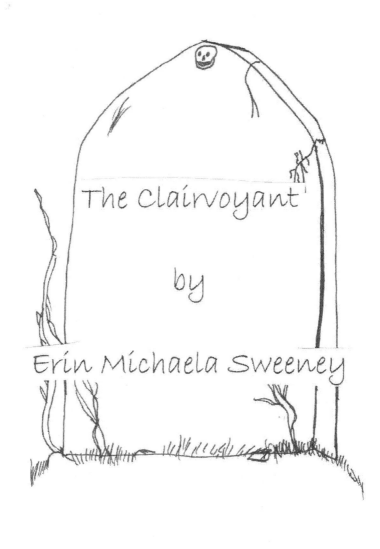

The Clairvoyant

by

Erin Michaela Sweeney

Karla never dreamed she'd be a widow at twenty-eight. How could it be—John was here one day and with the shriek of metal on metal gone forevermore?

More and more, Karla wondered whether grief had taken over her analytical mind. First she heard a Hindu goddess lament lost loves. Now she allowed a clairvoyant called Willow talk her into meeting at John's grave at midnight to try to contact him.

She pondered the two possible outcomes if the clairvoyant reached her dead husband. Karla might hear her own callous words repeated back to her. She shuddered at the remembrance of their final exchange—she too busy preparing for a job interview to even bother to wish him a good day, much less pour out her heart. And what if John did not communicate anything? Karla's visceral reaction to that possibility quickly led her to pass out momentarily from hyperventilating.

As the clock ticked toward the witching hour, Karla imagined a moonless night. Because the adjoining church held too much of her sorrow, Karla would make her way along the back path through tangled overhung tree branches to John's headstone. Her mind leapt to a petite blond in a flowing, shimmery white dress, beckoning to her with open arms. Karla wondered whether the clairvoyant would illuminate the séance with only blood-red, dripping candles.

Before Karla left their—no, *her*—apartment, she remembered Willow's instructions to bring three possessions: an object from John's childhood, one embodying his contentment, and something to signify his love. Karla pocketed his onionskin shooter, jasper mala beads, and platinum wedding band, and headed out the door.

She had buried John less than one month earlier in this graveyard. The marker made of unpolished granite had his full name, birth and death dates, and "Beloved Son, Brother, Uncle, Husband" etched into its solemn face.

Karla approached the ethereal Willow from behind and croaked out a greeting around the lump of sadness in her throat. The young widow, who stood head and shoulders taller than the clairvoyant, stretched out her hand. Instead of taking it, Willow gently drew Karla in for a warm embrace. The hug, which seemed to last forever in that moment, lightened Karla's tearful burden.

Willow's sapphire eyes glowed in the light of a nearly full moon, and she asked, "Did you bring the focus objects?"

"Yes," Karla replied as she slipped the keepsakes out of the pocket of her brown, hand-knit sweater.

Willow examined the three items in turn. First she held up the large, striped marble to one of the dozen glowing white pillar candles. Then she daintily brought the chunky, squared-off ring to the tip of her tongue. Finally, she closed her eyes and fingered the strand of 108 reddish-brown beads, whispering something to herself. Willow centered the ring on John's headstone, then balanced the marble atop the ring, and encircled them with the beads.

"Now, let us sit beside the headstone," Willow instructed, reaching for Karla's hands. "Close your eyes and say to him, 'I am here.'"

"I am here," mumbled Karla.

"Again. Louder."

Though she felt silly, Karla repeated the phrase.

"Keep going, more, more," urged Willow.

Karla repeated the phrase over and over until the words no longer made sense. They were simply sounds erupting from her mouth.

Suddenly, a bone-chilling wind blew through them, shivering the leaves of the oak trees, and Willow shook violently, releasing her firm handhold. Karla heard someone gasping in terrible pain.

Her eyes flashed open. With the candles no longer glowing and the moon shrouded in clouds, Karla sought out Willow's form, patting the ground nearer and nearer the gasps.

To her horror, she discovered the clairvoyant convulsing over sacred ground six feet above John's casket. Karla screamed.

In a moment of clarity, she searched her pockets with fumbling fingers, trying to locate her cell phone to call for help. No luck. Then Karla remembered she'd tucked her phone in the glove compartment. Running blindly toward her car, she stumbled over tree roots, branches scratching her tear-streaked face.

After calling in the emergency, Karla grabbed her flashlight to return to John's grave. She discovered Willow cross-legged next to the headstone, as if nothing had happened.

"Are you OK," Karla asked.

"Yes, of course," Willow replied.

"But you were gasping and convulsing and—"

"Sorry if I scared you," Willow interrupted. "I'm epileptic, and I sometimes have seizures when working."

"Are you sure you're alright? Because I called 9-1-1, saying it was an emergency. I imagine the—"

"I'm fine, but we should go." Willow quickly stood, brushing debris from the folds of her silk dress. She stepped toward Karla and gave her another hug.

Glancing past Willow, Karla realized the three keepsakes were no longer on John's headstone.

"Wait," Karla said, pulling away from the hug yet keeping her hands on Willow's shoulders. "What happened to the keepsakes?"

The clairvoyant gazed deeply into Karla's eyes. She then closed her eyes reverently, bowed her head, and uttered in another's voice, "They are with John now."

In amazement, Karla recognized the dulcet tones of Dhumavati, the Hindu goddess of lost loves.

***

The following morning, Karla called John's childhood friend, Derrick, to find out whether he could replace the gifted mala beads. Derrick sighed heavily at the enormous effort it would take to get out of bed, much less travel across the Bay Bridge to the little shop that sold the beads seven years ago.

"How did they go missing," Derrick asked.

Karla told her tale of meeting the clairvoyant in the graveyard. She included every detail from the previous evening except hearing the voice of the Hindu goddess. She treasured that moment too much to have Derrick sully it with one of his sarcastic remarks.

"You were duped," Derrick admonished and hung up on Karla.

She was left wondering whether Willow the clairvoyant was a fake.

Connection to the Other Side

by

Amanda Steel

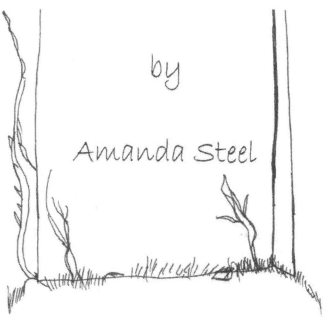

It started off as just another day, I was late as usual after spending half an hour straightening my unruly hair and of course it was raining and messing up all my hard work and I hadn't been able to find my umbrella. Then a car sped up as it approached, because there was a puddle.

"No, no, no!" I pleaded as I hurried to get past the puddle but I wasn't quick enough and I was treated to a shower of muddy water as I heard laughter from the car. "Thanks, just thanks, you bast-" I began as I heard a noise like a phone ring tone, but it couldn't be mine. I lost mine after Andrew's funeral. It was a month later and I still hadn't bought a replacement. It didn't seem important, I didn't want to be dealing with calls from concerned friends and family asking if I was okay anyway. Of course I wasn't okay, I had just lost the man I loved. The phone was still ringing, so I reached into my bag and pulled out an iPhone.

"What the…" I stared dumbly at the screen and it took me a few seconds to register the fact that it had the caller as 'Andrew', but it couldn't be, could it?

"Hello?" I felt stupid even thinking it could be him, on this phone which had just mysteriously appeared in my bag from who knows where.

"Cath, is that you?"

"Andrew?"

"Cath where are you?"

"On my way to work, where are you?" Well what else could I ask?

"I don't know I can't see, it's…"

"Oh my god, we buried you alive, you were pronounced dead."

"I don't think I'm buried, I can walk around, so I'm not in a coffin, it's just dark, like nighttime but with no street lamps."

Suddenly I felt so stupid again. 'Nice one whoever you are, you had me going there, you fucking jerk face, you sick…' I began but the phone went dead and since there was no longer anyone on the other end to take my rage out on, I launched the phone across the road and watched as it shattered.

An old man walked past and looked at me in disgust while muttering, "young people today, no respect for their property."

It was only when I got home after a long day of fake smiles and pretending to be okay to my work colleagues and started making something resembling dinner that I heard the ring tone again. I looked around in confusion. Where was it coming from, the fridge? I felt stupid as I opened the fridge, expecting to be confronted with almost out of date tomatoes and meat slices as well as having to face up to the fact that I was imagining things. But there it was, the iPhone and it was still ringing and claiming to be "Andrew calling".

"Who is this? It's not funny anymore," I shouted into the phone.

"It's me, it's so dark, where are you?"

I began to cry, "Andrew, is it really you?"

"Yes it's me, but I don't know where I am."

"Do you remember..."

"What?" he questioned.

"Do you remember what happened?"

"No I went out to get a newspaper and then I woke up here, wherever here is."

I cried even harder.

"Sweetheart, are you okay?" he sounded concerned.

"Am I okay?" I thought incredulously. He was the one who was dead, except he didn't seem to remember that. I felt like I should tell him, but what if he freaked out? What if he hung up and never called back? I couldn't lose him again. I wasn't even going to question how a dead person could get their hands on a phone.

"Yes I'm okay now I'm talking to you," I began.

"So what am I supposed to remember?" he asked. "I didn't forget our anniversary did I?"

"No you didn't forget," I assured him. "I love you."

"I love you too."

"Speaking of anniversaries, do you remember our first anniversary?" I asked.

"Of course, we went to that restaurant you liked in Dorset and you were wearing that light blue dress, with your hair in curls past your shoulders, it was blonde then and you kept smiling at me. I couldn't take my eyes of you, neither could half the men in that place. You never even noticed and I felt like the luckiest man alive."

I gulped and forced myself not to break down, I felt like throwing myself on the floor and sobbing until there were no tears left, but Andrew was on the phone and I just needed to keep him talking. I had to hear his voice.

"Are you still there sweetheart? It's getting cold here."

"I'm still here, I wish I could warm you up."

"I'll bet you do," he responded flirtatiously.

"Remember when we went to Scotland on that cheap holiday?"

"You mean in the middle of December," his voice sounded slightly happier again.

"It was freezing," I laughed "but we stayed in bed and kept each other warm."

"We worked up quite a sweat didn't we?"

I closed my eyes and could almost imagine I was back there in Scotland under the covers with Andrew, our bodies wrapped around each other, hot and sweaty in spite of the heavy snow fall and icy conditions outside our little rented cottage.

"Did you see that too?" he questioned. "It almost felt like we were back there."

"It did," I agreed and thought about trying something else. I thought about the time we had our first kiss. "Remember our first kiss?" I asked.

"How could I forget?"

"Really think about it," I encouraged as I fell silent and did the same thing.

I almost felt like I was 18 again and in Andrew first car. He was running his hand up my back and holding my hand with his other hand. He kept looking at me but it became obviously he wasn't going to kiss me first. So I leant in and I pressed my lips against his and began to taste his mouth. He pulled me closer and kissed me, passionately like he thought I might disappear, then someone appeared on the back seat. Wait that never happened.

"You can't stay here," the man told us, his face was covered with a hood.

"What? How did…" Andrew began, but then I found myself back in the kitchen. The phone was nowhere to be seen.

I looked everywhere in the kitchen, ripped out all the drawers, threw old tins of soup and beans out of the cupboards as I desperately tried to find the phone. Even though I had been in the kitchen when it vanished, I still checked the other rooms. By the time I was done everything was a mess, but I didn't care. I wanted to find that phone, I had to. It was the only connection I had to Andrew. Without it, he was really gone, but he couldn't be gone, not again. It seemed so harsh and cruel that this iPhone would magically appear, let me talk to Andrew, then vanish again. I thought maybe it was punishing me for throwing it across the road earlier that day.

"I'm so sorry," I wept, "I didn't mean to, I didn't know, please come back, come back, come back," I continued to repeat until my throat hurt and I curled up on the floor until I passed out from the exhaustion of all the crying and pleading.

When I woke up the phone was ringing again, I almost leapt off the floor with joy. It was coming from underneath a pile of clothes which I had emptied onto the floor earlier. I found it and shouted into the phone.

"Andrew, are you there?"

"I'm here, where did you go?"

"I'm so sorry I...I lost the phone, but I'm here now."

"Who was that in the car?" he sounded unnerved.

"I don't know, let's not think about him."

We talked for a few hours, recalling more of our happy memories, until the hooded figured appeared again, this time in a garden centre. We were picking out a tree for our first Christmas in our new home.

"I told you, you can't stay." He insisted.

"Leave her alone," Andrew stood protectively in front to of me as hooded man approached us.

"'Stop it," I began to cry again. "It didn't happen like this, you're ruining it, you're ruining everything."

"You'll be trapped here if you stay any longer," the man in the hood threatened.

"I don't care, this is where I want to be," I insisted.

"You heard her, go away." Andrew said, but the man kept trying to approach me.

I hid behind Andrew as he punched the hooded man, then reached for my hand and led me out of the garden center.

"Where are we going? Aren't we going to get a tree?" I asked, feeling like we were supposed to stick to how it happened the first time.

"We'll go somewhere else," he told me.

We drove in silence for hours before we arrived at another garden center miles away from home and I wasn't even sure where we were.

"Quick in here," he told me as the hooded man appeared across the car park.

"How did he get here so quickly?" I asked as panic rose up in me.

"I don't know but he's not going to take you away from me again, I know that because I won't let him."

"Take me away I'm not the one who..." I began.

A memory tried to form in my head, but I shook it away. "That man in the hood, I've seen him before," as another memory invaded my mind, this time of a graveyard. That had to be from Andrews's funeral, but I shook that away too. I didn't want to be reminded of that.

"I can't lose you again" Andrew insisted.

We ran, I don't have time to talk as we try to get as much distance between us and him.

We finally found a hiding place in between some of the larger Christmas trees.

"I'm sorry I don't have time to break this to you gently but you died," I gasped, "you went to get a newspaper and you were hit by a car."

"What?" he looked at me. I thought he was trying to process being dead but then he went on to say, 'that never happen Cath, it's true that I went to get a newspaper, that was the last time I saw you alive, because you went to work before I came back and you worked late. It was dark when you got off the bus and were walking home. That guy in the hood, he dragged you into the alley and…" Andrew couldn't go on.

"No."

"I'm sorry," Andrew told me gently as the hooded man approached and the memory of my ordeal which resulted in my eventual death flooded my brain.

"No," I said again as Andrew took my hand and led me away.

"We can't let him take you away from me again," Andrew said fiercely as we ran.

It was dark, but Andrew seemed to know where he was going.

I fumbled for a light switch and eventually found one, the room was lit up and there was Andrew lying on his bed with two empty pill bottles beside him.

"What did you do?" I demanded suddenly feeling angry.

"I couldn't live without you and soon I won't have to, see..." he pointed to his other self as his breathing seemed to slow. "I'm nearly gone, remember when we promised, at our wedding, together forever. I'm just keeping my promise."

"Not like this," I shook my head, "I never wanted this." I pulled away from Andrew as he reached for me. That's when I noticed the phone on his bedside table. It was like the one I had been talking to him on, right down to the slight scratch in the top right hand corner. I reached for it and dialed for an ambulance. I managed to tell the operator someone had taken an overdose and give her the address before the call cut out.

"What did you do that for?" Andrew accused.

"You'll understand someday when you're old and have children and even grandchildren, after you've lived a long and happy life without me," I tried to explain, but he looked betrayed.

The hooded man appeared, "It's time to go," he told me.

"Not yet, I just want to make sure he's okay, then I'll go with you." I had realized he wasn't really the same guy who had attacked me in the ally.

We both appeared at the hospital watching as the medical staff battled to save Andrews life.

"Why did you choose to wear his face? You must have known it would scare me?" I asked the reaper.

"I had to shock you, it's not uncommon for people not to realize they're dead, even to create elaborate lives like you did."

"You mean I could have created any imaginary life I wanted, but I choose to create one where I get splashed by puddles and everything is basically shitty.'

"You wouldn't have believed it if it wasn't."

I nodded, "So Andrew, that really happened? But he wasn't dead."

"Close to death, it happens sometime, some people at deaths door they could go either way, they slip the net and get a glimpse of the other side, now shall we go?"

"Just a few more minutes," I pleaded and he nodded in agreement.

"You know what happens if you stay too long?" he asked.

I nodded, I figured I would be stuck, beyond that I didn't really know, but I was sure it wouldn't be good for Andrew or me. He needed to move on with his life, but I was worried that he might try to end it again and I wouldn't be there to stop him.

The reaper seemed to read my mind. "That was just a fluke you shouldn't have been able to make that call to the emergency services. Even if you stuck around there's no guarantee you could save him a second time." He agreed to give me half an hour, but told me if I chose to stay after that, I would be stuck forever. "You've already been given a lot longer than most souls get," he insisted before vanishing.

I watched as the hospital staff worked on Andrew and discussed how he might just pull through and how lucky he would be if he did survive.

"Who made the call?" one questioned.

"A woman I think, from his phone, she must have found him."

"But the medics say there was nobody else there when they arrived at the house."

"Maybe she left?"

"That's so strange though isn't it?"

"You have no idea," I said more to myself than to them, as I knew they couldn't hear me but Andrew seemed to stir slightly at the sound of my voice. "Andrew? Please fight, live,' I pleaded. "I love you, I'll always love you, but you have to go on without me now, for me."

"Cath," Andrew mumbled.

"Try not to move sir, you took an overdose, but you're going to be okay," somebody said.

"Who's Cath?" a nurse questioned.

"Maybe the mysterious woman who made the call," another suggested.

Andrew's eyes were open and I thought he was looking right at me, he even seemed to smile as though he understood, but then he looked away. If he had seen me it had only last a few seconds, then the reaper appeared beside me again.

"I know, time to go." I said before he could say anything.

I took his arm as he led me away. I made a move to look back.

"It's better if you don't look back," he told me, "just look straight ahead."

I did as he suggested, he was the expert, and for me it was all new. I had no idea how long we had walked before I could no longer hear the sounds of the hospital behind us. I know it's a cliché, but there was a light ahead of us and the reaper told me to go into it.

"Really?' I asked.

"It's familiar," he reasoned, "everyone's heard of going into the light, it's actually a door, but you try saying go into the door, it just doesn't sound as dramatic and these days everyone wants a dramatic ending."

"You're not coming?"

"This is your journey not mine," he encouraged.

Without another word I walked cautiously towards the light and as I grew closer, I could see that it really was a door and the light changed and became Christmas lights decorated around a brown door. I remembered that door it was my front room I looked back to ask the reaper why my heaven or whatever this was appeared to be my front room. Instead of seeing the reaper I realized I was standing in my hallway.

"Well are you going to stand there all night?" Andrew asked as he stepped out of the kitchen, "everyone's inside waiting for the host."

I remembered the night, I had lived this. It was our first Christmas together. The tree we had picked was inside the front room and all our friends and family were sitting round it waiting to exchange presents even though it was only Christmas eve. I followed Andrew in the front room and even though I knew how this night went I lived every moment of it right up until the final champagne toast when my parents toasted to mine and Andrews' first Christmas together.

"Here's to many more," Andrew raised his glass.

I watched Andrew open his present from me. It was an iPhone, all new and shiny with no scratches or at least not yet. That's when I figured out that it wasn't a fluke, it wasn't even about me. It was the iPhone. It was magic. He didn't understand why I wanted to send a text message to the same number, but he agreed when I made him promise not to open it until it was five years later.

"It'll be broken by then," he reasoned.

"Just trust me and promise okay?"

"Okay," he agreed as I stood and typed out a message, while blocking his view.

"Yes it was me, so do what I said and keep going." I pressed send.

Andrew didn't keep his word and he read the message immediately. "What's that meant to mean?"

"Just save it and five years from now, it'll make sense."

The oversized oak door to the church sighed as the verger opened it. It was too heavy for the wind to whip it, but it fought in her hand all the same. Evie flipped the light switches and a darkness as black as midnight in the desert came over the church and the castle grounds where it was situated. She shook her head, and thought for the umpteenth time, what fool put the light switch in the church and not in the castle gates? She would now have to walk through the graveyard, then up through the castle in virtually impenetrable darkness. The winter moon, low and dim, created deeper shadows rather than helpful light. She looked up at the sky and watched as a cloud drifted across and blocked what little light there was completely. It created an even darker black, one where she couldn't even see her hand in front of her face.

"At least I have a torch on my phone," she muttered as she slipped through the gigantic door and out into the night.

She went into battle with the lock. It was nowhere near as ancient as the church itself, but it was old enough. She spent a good ten minutes wriggling and cajoling the key until eventually, with a loud clunk, the door was secure. She tucked her key back inside her pocket and looked out across the grounds. Not long, she thought, and she would be home in the warm, ringing the Vicar to let him know she was safe and watching her soaps. There was a wedding in one tonight and she had been looking forward to it all week, something was bound to go wrong. She hoped Lisa, the jilted lover, would turn up and put the cat among the pigeons.

She stepped out from the shelter of the archway and the wind blasted her, almost knocking her to the ground and ripping her hair out of its neat bun. It screamed around the gravestones and through every bone in her body. When it dropped momentarily between gusts, the quiet was chilling. She reached into her bag and dug out her phone, found the right button and turned it on. The screen flashed bright in the darkness and then a warning came up. Battery Critically Low. She pressed the button for the torch function, but it was too much for the dying phone to cope with. The screen flashed again and the word 'Goodbye' appeared before it turned itself off.

She tried not to swear too loudly as she shoved the phone back into her bag. She looked up and ahead of her stretched complete blackness. In the distance, what seemed like miles away, she could just see the faint orange glow of a streetlight that marked the entrance to the car park outside the castle gates. However, she had to negotiate the churchyard first, and then the quarter of a mile up the main thoroughfare, avoiding the deep pot holes in the road. Still, it gave her a vague direction.

A leaf, caught on the wind, slapped her in the face. Evie jumped and cried out, her voice not audible above the roar, but she heard it. Her heart thumped in her chest and her eyes darted about, not able to see anything, but desperately searching for some kind of reference point, something to ground her. She shivered; it was truly the back end of November now and the weather was gearing up for a long, harsh winter.

She realized that if she didn't get moving, fear would

overtake her and she would end up spending the night in the church. She started to walk, hoping she was keeping to the path and she wouldn't end up tripping over a gravestone or a fallen branch. The wind howled around the castle, echoing across the cricket pitch and into the turrets. She could feel the salt from the sea sticking to her face. It tasted fresh and bitter on her lips. It wasn't raining, but the castle was right on the shore, and the wind was picking up the sea water as it crossed the harbour and came into the grounds. The tide wasn't yet high, she could tell because of the intense smell of the moat; rancid, rotten and rich. It was always overpowering when the sea hadn't filled it. It was close though, high tide was due in an hour or two. Her coat was some protection from the arctic wind, but not enough. It made her even more desperate to get home to her warm cottage and a cup of tea. Or maybe a brandy for medicinal purposes.

She was almost at the kissing gate, the entrance to the churchyard, when she heard it. Footsteps. Behind her. The wind had lulled for a moment and she heard the shuffle of someone walking very slowly. She turned around, but everything was black or blacker, it was impossible to distinguish one shadow from another.

"Hello?" she called. "Who's there?"

There was no answer, just the whisper of the wind through the trees and the roses. She started walking again, aiming for the pale glow of light signifying the safety of Castle Street and the inhabited world beyond. She kept it just to her left in the hopes that would keep her on the path. Once she was through the kissing gate, she would try and keep the light in front of her for the walk up through the center of the castle grounds.

Again, she heard the shuffling of footsteps. It sounded like it was someone very old, maybe walking with a frame, someone who was not at all surefooted. She couldn't blame them in this dark, she couldn't see her own feet never mind where she was putting them.

Evie turned again, and the footsteps stopped. She thought she could hear breathing, dry and ragged, but it could just be the roses brushing against each other. She thought she could smell a cigarette, but there was no tell-tale burning ember. She put her hands out in front of her, searching the space as she would with her eyes, but she touched nothing. She turned again, took a hurried step forward and walked straight into the thick wooden support of the kissing gate.

"Bugger!"

Her bag fell from her shoulder and landed on a path with a crash. Her forehead seared with pain. She clapped her hand to it and started kneading with her fingers. It didn't help at all, but it was all she could think to do. A knot was already rising on her left temple. Her eyes watered and involuntary tears streamed down her cheeks, making her face feel like ice.

"Pull yourself together Evie," she said.

She bent down to pick up her bag, feeling first for the kissing gate. Her bag wasn't at her feet where she expected it to be. She felt around, as far as she could reach without moving her feet, but there was nothing. She shuffled in a small circle, running her hands over the stony path. She felt something smooth and round. At first she thought it was a pebble, then she realized there was ridge running around the edge. It was a shoe.

She stood up abruptly, her heart going nineteen to the dozen once more. It wasn't the first time she had met someone in the grounds at locking up time, but usually, they at least spoke.

"Hello?" she said.

There was no reply, but there was definitely someone there. She could sense them in the dark, touching distance in front of her and the smell was stronger, like an overflowing ashtray. She took a deep breath.

"Hello? Can I help you? I'm just locking up, so you'll need to leave the grounds now."

"Would you care to dance?" The voice was wheezy and like rubble.

"Erm, no, thank you, we have to leave now. Will you walk with me?"

The sense of someone being there disappeared, leaving behind just a faint whiff of stale smoke. She knew the man had gone, she just didn't know where. She hadn't felt him walk past her, so she assumed he had gone back into the churchyard.

"Excuse me!" she called. "You need to leave now. Please, come with me and we'll head to the gate."

Only the whoosh of the wind answered her. It was slowly gathering momentum again and building up into another squall.

She hissed in annoyance and reached down in an attempt to find her bag again. It was right at her feet; she wasn't sure how she had managed to miss it in her first search. She pulled it onto her shoulder with such force that she felt the strap give a little.

"What an idiot," she said.

She brushed her hand along the wood of the kissing gate to guide her through it, and went out onto the main thoroughfare. Only quarter of a mile to go and she would be out of the castle and on her way home. However, this last part would have to be taken cautiously, as it was littered with those ankle snapping pot holes.

She turned to face the glow coming through the distant gate and started to walk, pointing her toes first in each step, feeling the road for hazards.

She had only walked a short way when the wind dropped to nothing. The silence was penetrating. It slipped through every nerve in her body. She stopped for a moment, listening for any sound at all. Nothing.

She started forward, but as she walked, she noticed the sound of shuffling feet again, quieter than her own crunching steps. Someone was following her once more. She could hear the same slow, cautious footsteps that she had heard in the churchyard. She assumed it was the man who had asked her to dance. Fleetingly, she wondered why someone with such advanced dementia was out in the dark on his own, as that could be the only explanation.

"Hello? Sir? If you just follow the sound of my voice, you'll catch up to me and then we can walk the rest of the way together."

"Would you care to dance?" The whisper breathed softly across her face.

Her scream echoed around the castle walls. All that came in response was quiet, almost controlled laughter.

Acid rose in her throat. She began to run. Sod the pot holes, she thought, sod the old man. She ran as fast as she could, skidding on loose stones. The inevitable happened, her foot slipped into a crater and her ankle twisted. She landed hard on the concrete. Her cry of pain was cut short when her bag punched her in the side and she was winded.

Gasping for breath, she lay huddled on the floor. Her ankle was throbbing and she had no idea as to how close she was to the gatehouse. She knew it couldn't be that far, as she had run quite a way. She looked wildly around her, but the glow of light that had been her guide was gone.

Evie tentatively touched her ankle, the pain was delicious. It didn't feel broken, but it did feel as though she would need to rest it for a few days. She pulled her bag out from underneath her and realized that the strap had finally broken and that it was lighter than it had been. She had obviously lost some of the contents. She sat up and tried to steady her breathing. She was just being silly, she knew that. There was just some old and very confused man wandering around the grounds and she had nothing to fear. She had locked up the church and castle countless times and no harm had ever come to her. This night was no different.

She slowly got to her feet. Without the glow of the streetlamp outside the gate, she had no idea which way she was facing. Two directions would lead her to the edge of the road, she would feel the grass under her feet and know to walk along its edge. One way would lead her back the way she had come and would take her down past the church and to the sea gate. That gate was locked at four by the Heritage man and she wouldn't be able to get out that way. The final route would take her to the main castle gate and the comfort of Castle Street beyond it. She wouldn't have to walk all the way home, she could go as far as the pub and call a taxi from there.

She knew that the edge of the fields were close, the road

was only around ten feet wide, and so she started limping forward. When she thought she had walked far enough to hit the field and she still hadn't, she turned ninety degrees and started again. This time, she came to the grass. She felt the edge with her foot and hit the mound that rose at the side of the field, the one that ran alongside the church. On the Keep side, there were large stones, but the field was flat. She sighed with relief, she knew where she was. If she kept the mound to her left, then she would be headed in the direction of the castle gate.

Clutching her bag under her arm, she started to limp on. Each step shot pain up her ankle and into her calf. She didn't know how far she had walked. She hoped she was close to the gate. She tried to convince herself that it had to be just a few feet, maybe twenty.

"And only half a mile from there to the pub," she said aloud.

Laughter echoed around the castle grounds. There was no mistaking it for the howling of the wind, as that was still deathly silent. It was an icy laugh, like the cracking of a frozen lake. Evie stood still, holding her breath, trying to stop her teeth from chattering. She didn't dare turn around in case she lost her direction again and she didn't know where the laughter had come from; the sound seemed to be everywhere at once.

"Crazy old man, I'll have to call the police when I get to the pub," she muttered.

She took a step forward and walked straight into something solid.

"Would you care to dance?" This time, it was whispered gently into her ear.

Her scream tore her throat, it seemed to come from her very bones. She clapped her hand to her mouth, but another hand, a cold one, closed over hers and pulled it away from her face and away from her body. Another cold hand slipped around her waist and settled in the small of her back. She could feel it chilling her through her coat and jumper underneath that.

"Dance!"

She was dragged into a waltz, there was no music to keep time to, yet she was keeping time. Each step came to her as though she had been dancing all her life. In truth, the only time she had ever danced was at her wedding, when she and her late husband had revolved around in small circles, both of them feeling uncomfortable and insecure.

This was different, she was being led in a proper dance, whirling around, and every step she took seemed to be the right step. She never once stood on the stranger's toes, never once tripped. The pain in her ankle had gone, she felt as light as a feather. If only she could speak. Her voice had disappeared and there was another scream, a long, desperate, heart-ripping scream, stuck in her chest.

As quickly as it started, it stopped. She was left standing alone in the castle grounds, in the blackest night she had ever seen. Her ankle was yelling with pain, she felt shivery and faint. She was disorientated once more, not sure which way she had to go. The edge of the field that had been her guide was no longer there.

Anxiety overcame her, she felt sick to her stomach and could not stop shaking. Her teeth chattered together in an uncontrollable spasm. She took ten tentative steps in the direction she was facing, but found no grass verge, she turned ninety degrees and tried again, but nothing. She tried turning just a little bit and walking again but still, she could not find the edge of the road. Frantic, she hobbled as fast as she could in what she hoped was a large circle. The path beneath her feet crunched, but she could not find the grass verge. Panic rose like a physical lump that made her want to gag even more.

She knew the castle like the back of her hand, she had played in its grounds as a child; she had been on picnic dates by the moat as a teenager; she had spent her adult life in the community of the church. She couldn't understand how she was now in such a confusing situation, so lost and frightened, in a place she so loved.

Laughter reverberated around the grounds again. It was louder and had a quality to it that made her shudder. It was gleeful and satisfied, full of joy. For the first time since her husband had died, Evie began to cry, tears streamed down her face and her breath came in hitched gasps. She still couldn't tell where the laughter was coming from, not that it made much of a difference, but it added to the cruelty of it.

A small voice, quiet and sugary, spoke from somewhere near her elbow.

"You need to leave, come with me. Be quiet."

A little hand, cold and damp slipped into Evie's and began to tug, pulling her along the path. Evie decided to go with it. She was terrified, but she trusted that little voice. She walked along, trying not to make any noise. The person on the end of the hand was hurrying, getting faster and faster, it was all Evie could do to keep up, her sore ankle feeling worse with every step. She felt the ground underneath change, it became spongy and soft. She tried to stop, knowing that if she strayed from the path she would never find the exit.

"It's ok, I can find my own way from here," she whispered.

"Come."

Evie couldn't stop herself, she was almost jogging now, her feet fumbling to keep up. The ground beneath her tipped, and the little hand let go. She went tumbling down a steep slope, knocking her already injured head on a stone jutting out of the ground. With an almighty splash, she landed face first in the freezing, filthy water of the moat. She was dazed but the water woke her up with a jolt. The laughter bounced around the grounds again, getting louder and louder. It was like thunder overhead in a summer storm.

Weighted down with her sodden clothes, it was almost impossible to swim to the edge. By the time her hands touched the mud of the bank, she was out of breath and desperately tired. Her fight for survival still outweighed her need for sleep, but only just.

She clawed her way up the bank, digging her fingers and toes into the mud to push and pull herself up. Once at the top, she rolled over onto her back and shut her eyes. The temptation to give in and sleep there and then was overwhelming, but she wouldn't allow herself to succumb.

She had to fight to open her eyes again, and the first thing she noticed was that there was a star in the sky. The wind had returned in full force too, it pounded the castle walls and roared across the field.

She slowly got up, her clothes clinging to her made every movement an effort. She was shivering and chilled to the core. She turned her back to where she thought the moat was and walked forward. She tried not to think about the little voice and the laughter. She tried to pretend that she had imagined them. It stopped her from running in a blind panic and having another accident. After a moment or two, the grass turned into concrete and she was back on the main path. She turned so that she was facing the castle gate, keeping the flat field to her right so that the gate was where she knew it should be, and started walking. She had only taken a few steps when light shone brightly in front of her.

There were people, they had torches and they were headed her way. She could have wept with the relief. She shouted to them and waved her arms, but they didn't respond. They didn't even look in her direction. Their torches bounced around, beacons in the night. As they got closer, she realized they couldn't hear her at all, but they were looking for her. She stopped shouting and lowered her arms.

"Here's her bag, the strap is broken," a man said. She recognized his voice as that of the head teacher at the local school.

"She must be here somewhere, spread out, and someone turn on the lights."

One of the torches bobbed away through the darkness down towards the church. After a few minutes, all the lamps came on that lit the thoroughfare. Evie just stood there watching, silent. People, perhaps ten, were spreading out in different directions, waving their torches, shouting her name.

"She's here!"

Evie watched as a few of the men climbed down the embankment into the moat. She watched as they came back up carrying what looked like a wet roll of carpet. She watched as they knelt beside the bundle, trying to breathe life back into it.

She realized that it was her body. It was her sodden, broken and battered body.

Down by the kissing gate, in the weak lamplight, she could see the old man. A little girl with a wicked grin stood holding his hand. He tipped his hat before walking away back towards the church. The little girl looked back over her shoulder just before the corner then they went around the far side to where the oldest graves sat and disappeared.

With one final, immense effort, Evie willed herself to walk back to her body. She was exhausted. The head teacher was still pushing her chest and breathing into her mouth. Her head was tipped back and her face was a mess. She hoped that she wasn't too late. She closed her eyes and stepped into herself.

"Admiral Ohmie?" a young man's voice said from a few steps behind me, pitched low like I hadn't heard him jogging down the path through the monuments and mausoleums.

With my head bowed, my eyes closed, I smiled the sad smile of a hunter, a smile that had birthed too many ghosts over the years and expected to create a few more. My lips so dry, the sting of the desiccated Martian air on the back of my throat, my voice cracked like ancient bones left out in the sun too long on a sandy plain on some hell-hole inside the asteroid belt. "You shouldn't have tracked me down so soon, Donny."

"You shouldn't have ditched me and the rest of your security detail." His voice quivered with what I hoped was fear for my well-being, but I knew it was not.

I opened my eyes, squinting in the harsh light of the sun blazing down through the wispy clouds, through the grime caking the ill-kept dome. The air stank of the corroding, aging joints holding up the Ferro glass plates, the rusting fans pushing breathable atmosphere into the bubble, the stink of mold growing in the cracks of the stone shrines.

"A military graveyard is hardly public, Donny." The gravestones of my grandparents and my parents rested in the sandy, red dirt with no traces of flowers, the markers for my grandfather and my mom the hardest to look at, but for different reasons. Why didn't I think to bring flowers? "Can't an old woman come back to her home for the first time in half a century and pay her respects to those who made her what she became?"

"You have a lot of enemies, ma'am. They're offering a lot of money to end you. A lot of money."

I turned to examine him, standing in his Federation fatigues, fatigues like mine, with a blaster in his hand, the safety off, the generator hot, the barrel pointing at me. My heart sank, and I peered into his eyes, trying to reach into his soul to find the kid who had joined the service to put things right. "Money's rarely a good reason to do a thing."

"Sorry, I didn't get here in time to save you from those damned terrorists, ma'am," he chuckled.

"So that's going to be your cover story?" I asked. "You're going to kill me, and claim you didn't get here fast enough to save me?"

"Oh, I'll be wounded in the process." He shrugged, smirking, looking like he had the answer and everyone else were fools. "I've learned so much from you. It's been an honor, and a boon to my career, to work for you."

He raised the blaster to take better aim.

"Fire," I whispered, subvocalizing, staring into his eyes to watch that moment of hesitation, that moment of confusion before his head erupted and his lifeless body slumped to the ground. I shook my head touching my finger to my temple. "Nice shooting, Waggoner."

"My pleasure, ma'am," he said, his calm voice crackling in my head. "I'm always at your disposal for pest control."

I nudged Donny's headless body over to its back to get the filthy thing off the grave of a good soldier who'd died at my side 40 years before in the Battle of Asucar.

Damned waste.

The wind bellowed mournfully. Martha crawled deeper into the pile of blankets. A faint odor rose from the bodies of Ma and Pa, which lay crumpled by the fireplace. If it came down to it, Martha could drag the bodies into the fireplace and make a meal out of them. Hopefully, it wouldn't come to that.

From outside the window came a voice, low and garbled like static from a transistor radio. She peered through the thick yellow curtains. At first, she saw only a churning maelstrom of sand, waves layered upon waves. Then a man appeared, his thin frame bobbing to and fro in the wind.

"Sis," Martha called out. "Would you come take a look at this?"

Francine's head poked from her pile of blankets, a gopher surveying its surroundings.

"What is it?" she asked.

"It's some kind of man," said Martha.

"Well, whatever you do, don't let him in."

"Take a look."

"You said he's a man, right? What more do I need to know?"

"There's something different about him. I can't quite place my finger on it, though."

"Well, alright." Francine emerged from her blankets, making her way to the window. Walking took some effort from her now. Her skin sagged loosely about her bones like an oversize blouse.

"He looks normal to me," said Francine, though Martha could hear the anxiety in her voice. "I don't see what you're talking about."

The man moved closer and closer to the window, until he was standing right in front of it. Martha and Francine backed slowly away. The man pressed two palms against the window, imprinting bloody handprints on the glass. He shoved the window, and it crashed to the floor in a cascade of glass.

Martha tried to run but found herself hypnotized, unable to move her limbs like a mosquito trapped in amber. He narrowed his bullet-grey eyes in on her, a mossy substance clinging to his hair and coat.

"Come with me," he said, his breath a thick haze of swamp juice and dead rats. He gripped each of their arms, dragging them through the broken window. Once outside, they no longer had to move their feet as the wind carried them like kites along, dragging them through the fields of Beckton. They passed the hollowed-out skeleton of the house once belonging to the McKinleys. Inside, the corpses of Mr. and Mrs. McKinley lay slumped on the kitchen floor, a trail of blood leading to the stove.

At last they arrived at the graveyard. Martha had often ridden her bike down the path leading through the middle of the gravestones after school, despite her Ma's warnings that she would "disturb the spirits of the dead." She should have listened, she thought, just like she should have heeded the advice to wear the dust mask on her way to school three weeks ago. She had worn it when she left the house, but as soon as she saw that the other kids she passed weren't wearing masks, she took it off. That mistake cost her Ma and Pa. Francine had insisted it wasn't Martha's fault, that the dust would have come anyway. Something in Francine's eyes, though, told Martha that she was at least partly to blame.

The day after that unfortunate bike ride, school was cancelled due to the dust – permanently, it turned out. Since then, about four times a day, Martha experienced what felt like a rake passing down her throat, scraping the dust in a circular motion. Each time, she felt lighter and weaker afterwards.

At first she thought she was just imagining the hollowed-out feeling, but then, when she'd look in the mirror, she'd notice her pants sagging about her waist, arms reduced to candlewicks.

Like a contagion the thinness spread to the other members of her family. They said nothing, and when Martha brought it up, they looked at her like she'd lost her mind.

"A rake?" Francine had repeated, contemptuously.

After two weeks, they had to admit that something was wrong. The crops began to die, the cows, the pigs, and the chickens. Some keeled over in the middle of the field while others marched to their death in the alligator-infested swamp.

The man paused at a large gravestone. "Ronnie Sims," the inscription said. He'd died two years ago. Gripping the stone with both hands, the man uprooted it, revealing a tunnel underneath.

He lifted Francine by the hair, shoving her down the tunnel. Next, he plunged Martha into the blackness following Francine's echoing screams. Scratching at the walls, dirt filled her nostrils, caking her fingernails.

She tumbled out of the tunnel's mouth. Several feet away, Francine dusted off her dress.

"What do you remember from our karate lessons?" asked Francine.

"Not much," said Martha. "I'll try, though."

Then the man flew through the air, tumbling to the ground.

Once again, her limbs went into lockdown, her jaw glued in place.

The surroundings looked familiar—Nelson's Hardware sat quietly tucked away in the corner, while Doyle's Tools & More, with its bombastic orange façade, domineered over the street. Yes, it was Beckton, all right—but no dust appeared. Just up the street from Doyle's sat Patty's Good Times, the bar and grill which the mayor had shut down two years ago on account of it being too "rowdy."

They entered the bar, moving swiftly to the dark hallway at the back.

A room full of smoke awaited them. Patrons seemed to be actively avoiding this room, one group going so far as to walk to the furthest side of the wall as they passed, as if the residue from evil spirits lingering in the doorway would somehow infect them.

Inside the room, a man with a greasy mustache filed his fingernails.

"Ronnie," said their guide.

"A pleasure, Lewis," said Ronnie. "What brings you here today?"

"I've sucked the whole town dry."

"Jesus, already?"

"Listen, buster, now's not the time to be passing judgments. Do you want these girls or not?"

Ronnie looked both of them up and down, eyes narrowed in concentration.

"Yes," he said at last. "They'll do just fine."

"So do I get another city?"

"How about Beckton, 2025?" said Ronnie. "That one's still relatively untouched. As long as you bring me more specimens. Three this time."

"Getting a little greedy, aren't you?"

"You'll need a different entrance strategy this time," said Ronnie, ignoring his question. "B 2025 is far too advanced to be deterred by a little dust. Why don't you go as a lightning bolt this time? Only, instead of descending from the sky, you can go from the ceiling. They'll never see it coming."

"Brilliant," said Lewis. "Always nice doing business with you."

As Lewis left the room, Ronnie turned toward them and grinned, teeth as sharp as splinters.

"You arrived just in time for the ritual."

"Did you tell your mum you were staying at mine?" Mark said as he picked a blackberry and popped it in his mouth.

"Yeah. She won't check, she's too busy with her new fella."

"What's he like?"

"On the dole. Drinker. Kinda like the last one."

"Did you bring some batteries?" Mark knew Graham would appreciate the change of topic.

"Yeah, enough for the Walkman and the flashlight."

Mark shifted the weight of the rucksack on his back. He had the tent, torch, and matches, and had given Graham a list of what he wanted him to bring. He'd said he had everything, but Mark was sure his best friend would've forgotten something. He always did.

"Shit. You know what I forgot?" said Graham, as if some form of telepathy had jogged his memory.

"So long as it isn't the grub we'll be alright. I'm starving."

"Nah. I got sausage and bacon from the butchers and lifted a few slices of bread from ma Nan's pantry. I've gone an' left Lovesexy in the stereo at home. We'll have to make do with Purple Rain and Sign O' The Times."

Mark wasn't bothered. He wasn't a Prince fan, he thought he was a bit of a puff, and the little speakers Graham had for his Walkman made the warbling vocals even worse. He was more concerned with listening to the footy on the radio, so long as they could get a signal, and the batteries held out.

They'd been walking for a while since jumping off the bus at a stop that seemed totally pointless since it was in the middle of nowhere. Then again, the stop before had been at least five miles back, and the next was as far again, so it wasn't pointless for them. The conversation had been the usual; girls in general, footy, the girls at school, Arnie films, and how Paul Tyler and his mates were such a bunch of wankers. They hadn't talked about where they were heading, they'd spent the past couple of days talking about little else, but as they looked down into the valley for the first time both of them stopped and looked.

"There's the church," said Graham. "I'm surprised it's still standing. Look, half the tower's missing."

"And that's the house then? Right behind it."

"Of course it is. Can't see any other bloody houses down there can you?"

"Alright, no need to be cocky," grumbled Mark. He hated it when Graham cheeked him like that. Particularly when his friend was an across the board set three while he was set one for English and Maths.

"You're not too scared to camp down there?" The question got him a point back by questioning his friend's guts before his own were.

"No way. I'm looking forward to it after what Paul Carling saw."

"That's bollocks," said Mark, even though he whole-heartedly wished it wasn't. "This is the same nob who superglued his nostrils together remember, and ended up in hospital after eating toadstools. He's an idiot, and either made the whole thing up, or imagined it when off his head."

"Probably," agreed Graham, "but what if it's true? Thirteen naked women dancing around a campfire in the graveyard. That's six each and one left to keep the fire going!"

"Six each to do what exactly? He said they had the bottom halves of goats!"

"You need educating Marcus, you really do. I've got just the thing to broaden your horizons in my bag."

Mark turned his gaze from the abandoned settlement below, "What?"

"Two Fiestas and a Playboy hand-picked from my brother's stash. That's for later though. Come on. Let's explore."

Twenty minutes later they were on the valley floor. The roof-less Church, where a ghostly choir could apparently be heard whenever there was a full moon, had been explored, as had the churchyard. They'd also checked out the exterior of

Fryton Manor. All the doors and windows were boarded shut, and even though breaking and entering had crossed their minds it was a step into criminality neither of them were too keen on taking.

"Do you really think it's haunted?" asked Mark as he stood staring at the heavy boards that blocked the front door.

"What? A place called 'Fryton'? And with the history the place's got? Hell yeah it's haunted. Look around. The place is weird. Feels weird."

"That's because you believe all the crap people say about it."

"It isn't crap," said Graham petulantly, "I told you, my Grandad has a book all about the history of this area. The Church was built over a Druid mass-grave the local tribe dug after the Romans massacred 'em and there's been un-natural phenomena ever since."

"Un-natural phenomena? When did you swallow a dictionary?" joked Mark, but Graham was hitting his stride.

He'd been borderline obsessed with the place recently, and Mark hoped he wasn't planning anything stupid.

"Yeah, un-natural. Strange lights, big black dogs roaming the graveyard with glowing red eyes that appear and vanish at random, and Carling swears on his mother's grave he isn't bullshitting."

"Come on mate," said Graham, "it's a spooky place granted but people always make up stories about places like this. Doesn't make 'em true."

"It isn't just stories. The whole village was wiped out by the plague. They all died in Church, hiding, thinking God would save 'em. It's facts mate, all in the book. Not a single survivor and the bodies left to rot because no locals would come near and all the houses fell down. Them's the ghostly choir folks hear sure enough. Years later the manor was built with the stones of the old houses and burnt down twice. It was re-built a third time and used as an orphanage by some baby farmers who drowned the kids in the pond out back. Hundreds of people have died in some pretty gruesome ways on this patch of land, it's a ghost magnet. Anyway, we'll see tonight won't we."

Mark looked at his friend, his passion for the place typical of his interest in the darker parts of human history. It was the only academic topic he had any flair for, but even then the teachers at school repeatedly marked him down for going into too much detail about delightful topics like death camps and medieval torture devices. It was a fact that his coursework on Auschwitz was just as detailed, and considered, as the straight Students called him "20 Watt" on account of how dim he was normally, but even then he'd only got a D, and an accusation of copying.

"Come on, let's get the tent up before you start prattling on about the highwaymen that haunt the crossroads up near the bus-stop. You're starting to sound like the specky one off Scooby Doo."

By 11:30 Mark's bravado was starting to waver. He'd flicked through the Playboy but it didn't do much for him. He hoped it was his nerves, and not that he was a bit gay, but the thought of how he felt when Miss Wiggington wore one of her low cut blouses made him pretty sure he wasn't. Fryton had been eerie in the day, in the dark it was worse. The batteries Graham had brought were flat, the drink he'd made by mixing half an inch from each of the bottles in his Mums drinks cabinet had curdled because he'd put Baileys in it, and the sausages had ended up half burnt and half raw because they'd resorted to trying to cook them on sticks. Graham had forgotten the frying pan. As friends the situation was more amusing than annoying, but all the same Mark wished they were listening to the footy with a nice drop of drink and well-cooked grub in their bellies. As it was he felt a bit sick, which just made his nerves worse.

The fire had burnt down and though neither said as much there was no way they were heading into the woods for more sticks. Instead, they moved into the tent. With the flaps zipped shut the world outside seemed to press in on them. The sounds of the night were all around, the screech of an owl, strange rustlings in the grass, and every now and then the pitter patter of rain like miniature claws scrabbling to get inside. The temptation for Mark to suggest going home was almost overwhelming, but held in check by two important facts – there was no way he was going to let his mate accuse him of being scared, and they were a bloody long way from home with no buses until morning.

"You're quiet," said Graham.

"Yeah. Tired."

"Want another drink?"

"You can't drink that you need to eat it. I don't know how you can keep it down."

Graham took another drink, and grimaced "Neither do I, but if Mum notices I've taken it I'll get a right battering. I'm not taking that for nothing."

"Pass it here then, can't have you getting sick on your own."

Mark took a drink of the foul smelling, foul tasting liquid. He kept his lips together in an effort to stop the clotted cream floating on the top getting into his mouth. It burnt his throat as it went down, and burnt again when he belched.

"I need a slash," Mark said, "I may be some time."

"Hold it in mate, we can piss in this bottle when I'm done," said Graham, who was busy chewing on a chunk of curdled Baileys.

"Sod off, I'm not doing that. One of us would wake up in the night, forget, and take a swig."

"It'd probably taste better, and warmer. Besides, it's supposed to be good for you."

"What? Drinking your own piss?"

"Yeah."

"How can it be when it's the shit your body doesn't want in the first place? You don't half spout some bollocks. I'm nipping out, won't go far."

"Well don't piss on the tent, go in the graveyard."

"I'm not an idiot, and this whole place is a bloody graveyard," said Mark as he unzipped the tent, and headed outside. The next sound he made was a scream.

"You well and truly shit yourself. You see him Kim? Proper shit himself."

The fire was stoked up now, Mark and Graham sat quietly at one side, Kim and Gavin sat opposite.

"What do you expect when you creep up on somebody in the middle of the night?" said Mark in a surly tone. If he'd fancied going home earlier he was certain of it now, what should have been a bit of a laugh had become a laugh at his expense. He didn't like it one bit.

Kim and Gavin had introduced themselves once Mark had stopped hurling abuse at them for scaring the living daylights out of him. It turned out Kim worked for the owner of the land and her uncle, the bus driver, had tipped her off about "two likely lads heading down to Fryton with their camping gear". Gavin, her boyfriend, had been only too happy to head out with her and "give the cheeky buggers a bit of a jump." Unfortunately, the more lager Gavin drank the crueler his jibes were getting, and Mark was genuinely worried about how things might develop.

"Well, it's getting late," said Graham with an exaggerated yawn. "Time I turned in."

"Late?" said Gavin "It's five to midnight and you're sat outside a haunted house. He can't go to bed yet can he Kim?"

Kim said nothing. Whereas Gavin had got louder as they'd sat around the fire, she'd become ever quieter. Even to a youngster like Mark it was quite clear that he was the dominant party in the relationship.

"Then again, then again," said Gavin as he took another can of Special Brew from the plastic carrier he was keeping tight hold of and pulled the ring pull, "you could go to bed if you like." He took a drink, he wasn't sharing, "but since its forecast to piss it down I insist you sleep in the house. What do you say to that?"

Graham said nothing.

"How about you Mark? Tell you what, you go in the spooky old haunted house for ten whole minutes and you can have a can. Sound fair?"

"You're alright ta."

"Sure? It'd prove you've got some hair on your balls. That scream was a bit high pitched. You ain't one o' them half girl half boy things are y'? Go on, five minutes. Dare y'."

"No thanks."

"Not up for it?" another drink, "Pair of queers, that's what I think. Came up here thinking it'd quiet enough for a bit of experimenting did you? I could get Kim here to cure you of that little problem if you like, show you what you're missing?"

Nobody said anything. He could have been talking to himself, and his skin had taken on an unsettling orange glow in the firelight that was made even more demonic by the leer which flashed across his face as he rubbed Kim between her legs. She visibly tensed but Gavin either failed to notice, or failed to care.

"No? Not up for that either? Well, we can't sit here in silence all night, so I'm going to do you a deal."

"Leave 'em be Gav babe, let's head home."

The slap shocked not just Kim, who received the blow against her left cheek, but also Mark and Graham. Things had taken a turn for the worse and they were powerless to do anything about it. Gavin, Gav-babe, was nicely settled into his twenties and built like the sort of person who worked on building sites, all tanned, lean and muscular. They were just a pair of kids and a girl who would have stood up to her boyfriend already if she was going to at all.

"Shut up, silly cow. You lads have got all this to come you know. Women, can't live with 'em, can't live without 'em. That's what they say, and it's damn right." Gavin downed his can, crushed it, and opened another. Neither Graham nor Mark were Special Brew virgins, they'd drank the odd can themselves down the park, but the odd can was the best they could manage. At 9% Mark's dad called it loopy juice, and the time Mark had managed a third can he'd spent the night hugging a porcelain girlfriend with a wide mouth and swirling throat. Gav-babe was on his fifth can that they knew of, and been swaying when he'd arrived.

"So, you won't go in the house, and I can't be arsed busting into throw a pair of pansy's like you two in there just to get sent up here tomorrow to board the place back up." He took out another can and passed it to Kim.

"I'm driving."

"It's not to drink y'daft tart. Put it on your cheek to cool it down. People think you're such a clumsy bitch the number of times you end up telling 'em you've walked into a door.

"So here's a dare. You two gaylords swim across the pond out back and we'll be on our way. I'm nearly out of beer as it is. How about it?"

"No thanks, I can't swim," said Graham.

"It ain't optional I'm afraid. You can bloody doggy paddle can't you? Now take that swim or I'll give you a slap as well and then chuck you in. And don't even think about trying anything, I do karate."

Gav dropped into an un-convincing pose that Mark guessed came from repeatedly watching Enter The Dragon than any martial arts training, but he wasn't about to put his suspicions to the test. "Come on Graham. It'll be fine."

"Like he'll go even if we do it," said Graham, his tone leaving Mark wondering if his friend was going to give it a go and lunge over the fire at their tormentor.

If he had been thinking of it then the thought was soon put out of his head by what Gav did next. He sat down, pulled up his trouser leg, and removed a Rambo style combat knife. "I'm waiting."

The pond was smooth and still as they slid into it wearing nothing but their underpants. A shining disk of obsidian blackness behind the over-looking manor house.

"This is where they threw the babies," said Gav as Mark and Graham sank deeper into the water. It was a sharp drop off, and they were soon down to their shoulders.

"Go on babies. Take a swim. Reach the far bank and we'll be gone by the time you swim back."

Kim stood a little further back, her arms clasped across her chest. Gav had taken his last can from her, it hadn't done a thing to stop the swelling which had blossomed into a purple rose across her cheek. Mark looked back and thought he saw a tear run down her face, a slight wet trail which glistened in the moonlight like a sliver of mercury, but as he looked she turned away and walked back towards the house, and presumably the fire at the other side of it.

It was cold in the water and soft underfoot. Suddenly Mark began to shake, fearful that he was treading on the soft, rotten, corpses of the babies drowned in the pond, and not just mud and silt which had built up over the years. He stood on something long and thin and gasped. Was it a stick? Or the bone of a small child? A child whose mother had paid for its care just for the owners of Fryton Manor to take the cash and then throw it into the pond? He was shivering and starting to panic, his breathing coming in short, sharp, shallow, bursts that were failing to get enough oxygen into his body. Graham was half way across the pond by now but looked to be struggling and, as Mark watched, he stopped and slid under the surface.

Mark started to swim. Graham bobbed up, down, up, then down again. Mark's muscles were burning and his vision was turning black. Graham hadn't come back up again. Gavin was shouting "Kim, Kim, get back here." Mark was now at the point that he'd last seen Graham. He reached down. Nothing. He stuck his head under the water but couldn't see a thing. Panic now had him in a grip every bit as icy as the water that surrounded him. He reached down again. Nothing. He dove down, blind, waving his arms side to side. There, a hand grabbed his, but it felt small. Too small. Smaller than Graham's should have felt even though they weren't in the habit of holding hands. He started swimming up but then another hand grabbed his other wrist. Pulling him down. He kicked his legs, trying to drag Graham back up with him. It had to be Graham, had to be, but it didn't matter. He didn't have the strength. Graham's weight, it was Graham, it was, pulled him down. His breath was spent, he was sinking. Darkness surrounding him. Darkness consuming him. He felt another hand grab him by the hair but it was too late. He was too heavy. It was too dark. It was time to sleep amongst the babies in their watery grave.

"You text your 'rents?" asked Aidan as he tapped away at his Blackberry.

"Yeah, said I was staying at yours."

"Nice one bud." They high-fived.

"So you Googled this place last night?" Aidan smiled as he said it. He knew his friend would have been on the net as soon as he'd suggested they camp the night at "Frightening Fryton - England's Most Haunted Deserted Village".

"Yeah, there's all sorts of weird shit about it."

"Told you. You read about the druid pit under the Church?"

"Yeah, and the plague. Nasty shit that."

"Not as fucked up as what went on at the Manor though."

Jasper stopped, they'd crested the hill and were now looking down into a valley which housed a ruined church and an ugly square house – Fryton Manor. "Yeah, that's dark. Charging people to care for their kids and then bashing their heads in and throwing them into the pond out back. Sick man."

Aidan stood by him, "Totally. And there's the two kids what drowned a few years back, and the lass who drowned trying to save them. Apparently she haunts the place now, beckons people out into the pond at midnight."

"Why'd she do that if she died trying to save people?"

"Fucked if I know. Could be she's summoning her boyfriend, my Uncle Pete reckons he hung himself in the Church tower 'cos he couldn't get over losing the love of his life."

"Your Uncle Pete said he'd been abducted by aliens. Come on, let's explore."

Graveyard Watch

by

Gweneth Leane

"I had better fill up with petrol or we'll be walking," my husband, Bruce, remarked pulling into a service station. Our plan was to visit the graves of my parents. I had not visited my mother's grave since she had been placed there two decades ago.

The cemetery as I remembered it was a scene from Wuthering Heights, gloomy and spooky. Centuries of Cornish miners and their families were buried there along with a ghost or two.

My feelings about my mother were ambivalent; our relationship had not been a close one more of an arctic freeze. Because we were touring in the area I felt obligated to pay my respects. I was a little afraid she might roll over and want to know why I hadn't visited her sooner.

Bruce returned to the driver's side to the car after paying for the petrol, disorientated.

"What's wrong?" I was alarmed. Bruce had a history of taking ill when we were touring.

"I feel really weird, I couldn't write my name and I can hardly walk."

"Ok, we are going to find a doctor," I said decisively. We eventually found a hospital, after hours of waiting Bruce was x-rayed.

"I feel OK now, there's nothing the matter with me," he said perkily, sitting up.

I was ready to commit a murder.

"You have had a mini stroke," the doctor pronounced, "rest is what you need."

Visiting Mum's grave was forgotten in the panic to find a medico. The visit was deferred yet again. "Forgive me Mum," I whispered. "I'll catch up with you sometime in the next decade or two. Meantime, have a happy RIP."

We planned to return home next day, cutting short our holiday just in case Bruce took ill again. My mother though, was not going to be relegated to the past not without a fight. She rolled over.

"You've always been a disappointment to me, you've always done exactly as you please.' her face was tight and lips pursed in discontent. Hair pulled into a tight bun at the base of her neck. I could hear her disapproving sniff; she stood at the end of my bed.

"But Mum ..." I sat up, what was she doing here? In self-defense, I enumerated all the things I had achieved in my life. I felt swamped with a familiar sense of failure.

I came awake as Bruce dug me in the ribs, "Wake up, what are you crying about?"

"Mum just rolled over in her grave because I haven't visited her," tears rolled down my cheeks. "Nothing has changed; she's as hard to please as ever. I never did anything that pleased her."

"Rubbish, it's just a dream." Bruce swept everything aside with the careless logic of a man. "She's been dead and buried for years, get over it."

Heads

by

Rod Martinez

"Heads, we get married; tails we break up. That was what we agreed to, right?"

He stood tall, looked down at her. Kim was easily the most beautiful girl that David had ever met, inside and out, but in his mind their relationship had moved way too fast for his comfort. And he remembered the last fight they had, she walked out on him, in the rain, in the dark. That night he had considered it his sign, he wiped his forehead and sighed, content that it meant he wouldn't have to take the plunge, tie the knot, be a victim of the old ball and chain as the guys kept chiding him about.

He stared at her, she didn't even budge. He held the practically new quarter in his hand. It was an almost new 2012 coin; he had kept it as their token of love. On their first date, it was given as change at Dairy Queen after their first ever sundae together and the coin was minted the year that they met. She said "Let's keep it, years from now we can show our kids that it was a sign, we had ice cream and the change we got back signified our first date, a nickel – five cents, fifth day; a dime - ten cents and the tenth month of October – then the quarter which was made in 2012."

He smiled thinking back on that moment as he stood near her on this hot Florida day, a slow sweat started on his brow. Kim was a Florida native; David came from New York. Truthfully, he knew that all his life he would probably never again find anyone like her, but being a guy and naturally fearing the commitment of marriage, he thought he'd just get away with stalling it just a little while longer. He looked at her, she didn't say a word and her eyes were closed and looked like she just might even cry. But no, he knew she wouldn't cry, or would she?

He held the coin out, looked at it, the glimmer from the sun bounced off his face and the tree next to him. David exhaled a nervous one, then, then it almost looked like he was choking back a tear that might form.

"Honey, I'm sorry," he shook, "... I uh, well you know how it is with guys, look at your brother Larry, he didn't get married til he was forty and he was dating Tonya for seven years!"

She didn't reply.

He dropped his face, for the first time in a long time; David Guzman didn't know what to say. He stroked her cheek.

"Baby, I'm sorry."

He closed his eyes, yes a tear was going to start, he wanted to fight it, but he couldn't. He couldn't because he revisited the night that she walked out on him after the fight. He had tossed the coin in the air and said "Heads, we get married; tails we break up."

It landed in her angry fist. She was so upset at his joke that she furiously ran out on him and walked right out into the thunderstorm, without an umbrella or even her purse. She just walked out into the night and only twenty paces out, got hit by the car she didn't see, and died on her way to the hospital, all without him knowing because he ran to get his umbrella then ran out to chase her the other way.

Kimberly Donovan was DOA when she got to Tampa General Hospital and it was her brother Larry that called him to let him know. When he made it to the hospital, he ran in and she was lying on the stretcher and her hand slowly opened …the quarter was sitting there, showing heads up.

"Heads… we get married." He sighed in tears as they started to close the top of the casket. Kim lay in state at the cemetery after all family and friends had left. David needed to have these final words. The cemetery worker walked up behind him.

"Sir, we have to close the casket and inter her." David turned to him, nodded, tears flowing from his eyes. He leaned over, kissed her, and then placed the quarter on her lips.

If I hadn't decided to go out into the garden that day, things would have been a lot different. If I hadn't woken up, drank my morning tea, and looked out into the overgrown weeds, thinking – *it's about time I fixed that shabby-looking jungle* – I'd have been saved.

But as it was, Kathy had been dead and buried seven months now, and I woke up that morning, suddenly realizing how much I had neglected my family home. So, stripping off the cobwebs and dust, I found my garden shears, my strimmer and the lawnmower, and I began my work.

My wife and I had lived in this house for almost thirty years. We had raised two children here, who had long since left. I had nursed my wife when she got sick, and when she died, I arranged the funeral. I looked after everything. And by the end of it, I was exhausted. I'd looked around the empty house, and the mere thought of having to maintain its cleanliness filled me with an exhaustion sharper than the sleepless nights towards the end of my wife's life.

My wife and I hadn't always had the perfect marriage, God knows I wasn't the perfect husband, but we got through it, we always did. I'd had a few...indiscretions along the way when I was young; the children were small and we weren't being 'marital' as such anymore. But after the event, my wife's face would creep back into my mind, hurt and crying, and I would slink back to the house before she suspected. Which was why, when my wife betrayed me, fifteen years ago, it was so much worse. That was why I had to go to such extremes, to teach her that she couldn't do that to me. But she learned, and since then we had been happy. I loved her after all, and she loved me.

At the bottom of the garden there was a huge patch of long grass, and weeds that had grown over it, intertwining. I had to cut back the weeds before I could use the lawnmower, so I bent down onto my knees, straining as they couldn't hold my weight the way they used to, and reached out to take a bunch of weeds in my gloved hand. There was an extremely dense part of the growth, as though in that spot, the weeds grew best. I pulled all the sticky, thorny plants back, and hacked and cut and trimmed until they too were suitable for mowing. But as I reached down to pull some long dandelions out of the ground, I saw something that shouldn't have been there. Something hard and grainy, like concrete. Was it an old stepping stone? A slab of brick that I had never noticed before? I pulled back more weeds and peered closer.

There's writing on it.

I read the words, and fear grew inside me like a cancer. It lodged in my heart and held on tightly, so I couldn't breathe. *Is this some sort of joke? Who would do this to me?*

I looked around to see if anyone was watching me, but there was nobody else around. The words spelled out a name: Thomas Jacobs. There were dates underneath it: 14 March 1952–17 September 1999.

It was a headstone, buried in the ground.

But that wasn't what scared me.

What scared me was the fact that I knew this man, my wife knew this man, my wife knew him well. But more than that, what shook me deep in my aging bones, what froze my blood in my veins was that this was the man my wife had had an affair with.

And I had murdered him for it.

My first instinct was that someone knew my dirty secret, and they had made this headstone and placed it here as a warning, or a joke. But other than my wife – who had known? Nobody, I was sure of it. No one else was there, no one else was involved at all.

I had stabbed him after I found him in my bed with my wife... I stabbed him so many times... we rolled the corpse up in the carpet we had in the living room, took it to the forest, and buried it. He was reported as missing, and the police held an investigation, but we waited, silently, and nothing ever came of it. I let my wife mourn her lover, and mourn him she did, for a while. And then it was over, we washed our hands of it, and we never spoke of it again.

Why would someone confront me about this now? All these years later?

But no one had discovered my secret. It was so much worse than that.

That night I didn't sleep well. I dreamt of Thomas, I dreamt of him and my wife, in my bed together. He was on top of her, groaning, she was beneath him, her legs spread, her arms...It was all playing out again, but instead of grabbing him and throwing him off her and beating him to a bloody pulp, all I could do was stand there. He turned to me, expecting my presence, and he smiled. It was a dark, knowing smile. He opened his mouth, and suddenly thousands of bugs crawled out and down his chin, down his chest, through his hair. All the while he continued to...I felt sick, but I couldn't look away. The bugs travelled down over the bed and dropped onto the floor, so many of them. They came towards me. I tried to run away, but my feet were stuck to the floor like glue. They crawled up my trouser leg, up my waist, my torso, my face, and crawled into my own mouth. I tried to scream, and batted my face. But there were too many of them; they were like a black, crawling sea. I felt them on my tongue, running down my throat, making me cough. I fell to the floor, and the last thing I saw was Thomas, his gaze still upon me, still smiling.

I woke up tearing at my throat, spitting out what I thought were bugs, and it took me a moment to realize that it was a dream. I inhaled sharply, deeply, grasping for air, and exhaled again. Inhaled, exhaled, calmed myself down. *It was just a dream, that's all. Just a dream.*

Even so, I was compelled to check out of my window, to make sure that Thomas wasn't standing outside somewhere, waiting for me, watching the house. I pulled back the curtain, and gazed out into the darkness. Nothing.

I slunk back into bed, ignoring the ringing in my ears, and closed my eyes. I tried to think of normal things, like what things I needed to buy from the shops, how to continue with the garden, whether I should even carry on with it at all.

I awoke naturally at 8:15am, and the first thing I did was go back out into the garden. Perhaps the stone wasn't there after all, maybe it was just my imagination, or my eyesight failing. I bent down into the bushes, and peeled back the weeds. *Gone, the stone was gone.*

It was my imagination after all! There was just a patch of normal-looking grass, nothing to distinguish it from the rest of the garden.

Relief flooded through me, and I sat back on my heels. I clasped my hands together, and smiled, looking around, shaking my head at my own silliness. I decided to get dressed, go to the shops, and treat myself to a fancy dinner. Perhaps some wine to go with it; I felt like celebrating.

I turned back towards the house, and marched triumphantly to the back door. But I suddenly tripped over a stone, hidden in the long grass. I twisted my ankle, and couldn't stop myself falling to the ground. I looked back, and saw what I had tripped over. *No.*

It was Thomas's headstone. *It's moved!*

Or someone had moved it. Someone playing with me. Someone who knows.

It was a warning, I was sure of that now. Someone knew what I had done, and they weren't about to give up harassing me. I would have to find out who it was, and silence them before any of this came out. I wasn't about to spend the last years of my life locked up in prison. *But hang on, what was that?* There was something else in the ground, something poking up near the stone. Something red, like rough fabric, patterned.

A rug. Our old living room rug. The one we rolled his body up in before we buried it. It's following the headstone. Coming towards my house.

That night I dreamt of Kathy. She was young again, and her curled, blonde hair bobbed beautifully in the breeze, her green eyes glowing with happiness. I loved her so much, and to lose her in such a way, was unbearable. I hated that I couldn't do anything to help her. I was her knight in shining armour, I was meant to have saved her from it all. But in the end, nothing went to plan, and she had died, all too late. In my dream, I had saved her, and we were on a beach together, enjoying the sun, drinking wine, enjoying each other's company. She was talking about mundane things, but it was the mundane things I loved the most; the everyday, the boring. I was smiling and sipping my wine, looking out over the beautiful sea.

But suddenly something appeared out of the water, and bobbed along its surface. Dark hair, a head, shoulders, a torso. *Thomas.* He rose out of the water. He was dirty, blood-soaked, his face slashed. His eyes were black with rage, and hate, and he moved effortlessly through the water towards me. Beside me, Kathy continued talking, smiling, she hadn't noticed that he was there. I had to get away, I had to disappear, to run and never look back.

I woke up again, shivering, in a cold sweat. The house was silent, but the silence was deafening; it hurt my ears. It was still dark, but I had to check the headstone, I just needed to know where it was.

But I didn't make it into the garden. I didn't need to, because the gravestone had crossed the threshold and was now in my kitchen. The tiles had been bunched up and broken in a line that originated from the back door. It was the rug, it had disrupted the earth underneath the house, and had broken the tiled floor. And standing beside it, his dark eyes blazing with hate, was Thomas.

He's come for me at last.

I turned and raced as quick as my stiff knees would carry me up the stairs. I ran into my room, and slammed the door shut, gripping my chest to still my heart. I stumbled over to the windowsill, and unlocked the window with shaking fingers. I expected to hear Thomas coming up the stairs behind me, I expected to see him burst through the door, to grab me and drag me away. But the house was silent, and after a while I wondered if I had imagined the whole thing.

But then I heard something in the kitchen, but it wasn't footsteps. It was a loud, dragging, thumping noise, and grunting. *What is he doing down there?* The grunting continued, and the occasional low thwack of something hitting the floor, and then the heavy dragging. I heard the familiar noise of the first step on the stairs being stood on. *He's coming up the stairs.* The next step was stood on, then there was another grunt, and a bump, like he had dropped something, or hit something against the carpet. He was coming, but so slowly that it calmed my nerves a little. I had more than enough time to climb out the window and into the night.

I climbed onto the windowsill, and looked out over the roof. The night breeze was cool on my hot face, and I breathed it in. I brought my leg up to the ledge, panic overthrowing the creaks and cracks I felt as I lifted it up, and accidentally knocked something over. I looked down. It was a photograph of Kathy, only a few months before she died. She looked as beautiful as ever, and so happy. Perhaps I should let Thomas kill me, then at least Kathy and I would be together again. I heard Thomas reaching the top of the stairs, and with panic steering me forwards, I went out into the night, on top of the roof. I looked back at the window and to my shock he was already there, standing inside my room, looking out at me. His face was twisted into a scowl, and he reached out a dirty hand towards me.

"Leave me alone!" I yelled at him, before turning back to make my exit. I just needed to land the right way, and I would be fine. Just jump down, and face the damage head on. I turned again to see if he was trying to climb out onto the roof, but he had disappeared from view.

I heard him clunking back down the stairs. I had enough time to beat him to it, and run away before he got to me. *Just jump, just do it!*

I leapt down off the roof, my heart in my throat, and braced myself for impact. As I landed, my leg twisted against the uneven ground, and snapped. Pain shot through me, an unbearable, sharp pain that I thought might cause me to pass out. I screamed, and clutched the broken bone. I could feel it jutting out underneath my skin, but there was no time to tend to it now, that would have to wait.

Because Thomas was back in the garden. And the thing he had been dragging around, was the rug we had buried him in.

"Why?" I yelped, pitiful. "Why are you doing this?"

He looked at me then, and I could make out the hatred he felt for me emanating from his eyes, even in the darkness. I knew why, of course, because I killed him. Because I did what I had to do to keep my wife with me. But that was fifteen years ago. Why all of a sudden does he want revenge?

"You killed her."

"What?"

"You killed Eleanor."

My wife. How does he know that?

"I don't know what you mean!" I yelled at him. "She was sick, she died from..."

"You poisoned her!" Thomas's large, dark form came closer, he used his right hand to pull the large, dirty, rotted rug up behind him, grabbing onto its very edge. With his other hand he grabbed my throat, and lifted me up. My broken leg swung loosely, painfully, and hit my other leg, sending shooting pains through my entire body.

"Please..." I whimpered. "Please let me go..."

"There's only one place you're going." He threw me to the ground, and watched me as I struggled to get away. I couldn't stand up, so I tried to grab tufts of grass to pull me out of the way. But Thomas was soon on top of me. He'd left the rug to the side behind him, and he now had me with both hands. He grabbed me again and brought me up to his face, so it was inches from mine. Immediately I smelt his decomposition, the rot and putrefaction of his body. His tongue was black, his eyes had rotted away leaving only the sockets, his skin was grey, and coming away like wet wallpaper. I struggled against his large frame.

"You killed me," he wheezed.

"I know Thomas, I was there," I replied sarcastically. "That's what you get for sleeping with another man's wife. In his bed no less!"

"You killed her. Why?"

"Why?!" I screamed back at him. I pushed him away and he fell to the ground. *Because of Kathy. You killed Eleanor because you wanted to be with Kathy. You thought that once your wife was out of the picture, you could play the part of the poor, grieving widower, and you could live happily ever after. But you weren't counting on that car, that car that hit Kathy at sixty miles per hour as she crossed the road. So you ended up with no one, on your own.*

"You never deserved her," Thomas breathed at me.

"But she stayed with me, didn't she? She kept our little secret. So really, you never deserved her either."

A low growl started in Thomas's chest, and escaped through his black lips. He leapt for me again.

"She loved me!" he screamed. He pulled back his arm, and then all I saw was his rotting fist come straight for my face. I was blinded by the pain. My lip burst and I felt something pop in my mouth. *My jaw.* Bits of Thomas's skin came off on my face, slid off his knuckles and stuck to me like the worst kind of glue.

I went to try and attack him. Maybe if I killed him again he would go away. But despite being dead, he was incredibly strong, and he batted my arms away. He then picked me up, and suddenly I realized why he had been dragging that disgusting rug around. He was going to put me in there, bury me alive.

Thomas threw me on top of the rug and my leg hit against the ground. I screamed in pain again. He leaned over and glared at me one last time before rolling me up in the disgusting rug. It was so heavy that I couldn't lift my arms against it, and I could only kick with my one good leg. I could see the night sky, only the top half of my face poking out, and I took one last, longing look at it before I was dragged away. I was pulled across the garden, and a few seconds later everything went black. I couldn't breathe. Blind panic filled me, and suddenly the pain in my leg and mouth were gone. I tried to scream but all I got was mouthfuls of dirt. All the while Thomas continued to drag me forwards. He had somehow known what I'd done to Eleanor, and for some reason he was okay with me murdering him, but not murdering her. Suddenly I hated my wife more than I had ever hated her before; this was her fault, the stupid bitch. If she hadn't cheated on me with that... with that, *drip*...I wouldn't have had to do what I needed to do.

I couldn't see Thomas, but I could feel his gnarled hand clutching my good foot, and his grunting as he continued to drag me down. We were underground, coming through a tunnel that Thomas must have used to dig his way to my garden. But where was he taking me?

Oh God, I know where we're going. The woods. Where we dumped Thomas's body like it was little more than a pile of manure.

All I could think about now was trying to keep breathing, to stay alive, to wait until he was gone and then try and dig my way out. But it was a long way to the woods, over an hour's drive in the car, and I felt my lungs bursting for air already.

I'm not going to make it; I'll die here.

My last thoughts were of Kathy, my beautiful, sweet Kathy. I'd loved her for years, and the affair we'd had only sustained us for a while; eventually we wanted to be together as a couple, but I knew Eleanor would never divorce me – there was too much she could threaten me with. So I'd started putting doses of insecticide in her tea, and it took a few tries to get it right. The first dose wasn't enough, and only made her sick. The second worked, and I'd rang Kathy, ecstatic with the news. But Kathy never answered her phone, and a day or so later I found out why. She was killed instantly at least; at least there was no pain.

I inhaled another mouthful of dirt, and tried to swallow it down so I could breathe. But another one came, and another. I tried to get rid of it; spit it out, swallow it, but there was too much as we went deeper and deeper into the tunnel. I didn't have the energy to scream anymore, I just needed to breathe, but there was no air.

Around three minutes into the journey, I finally stopped breathing, and Thomas dragged me the rest of the way in silence.

Two bodies were found in Starley's Forest yesterday morning. One of them, little more than a skeleton, was identified as the body of missing person Thomas Jacobs. The other body was fresh, barely decomposed, and was identified as Paul Cooke. A large amount of soil was found inside his throat and stomach, and he had sustained a broken jaw and broken leg. Both bodies were wrapped inside a large rug. The strange thing about this find was that Mr. Jacobs's fingers were wrapped around Mr. Cooke's leg, and it took a pair of pliers to pry the fingers away. The fingers broke off in the process. We placed the bodies in the morgue, but someone must have made a mistake.

Because although it was reported they were placed in separate drawers, they were found inside one, together, inside the same black bag. Mr. Jacobs had been placed in such a way that it looked as though he was holding Mr. Cooke down. His bony fingers were placed around the other man's throat, his other, fingerless hand placed against his chest. It was obviously someone's idea of a joke, either that or we just didn't have the rigorous recruitment process that we used to.

As I looked at them both together, shaking my head at my staff's incompetence, Mr. Cooke's body suddenly convulsed. Despite my professionalism, I shrieked and fell back, waiting for the corpse to fall to the floor, or worse...get up and start moving. I had no idea how much time had gone by before I gathered the courage to stand up again and take another look. What I saw shocked me.

The skeleton of Mr. Jacobs was now lying flat on top of Mr. Cooke, as though he was holding him down, stopping him from getting away.

Over the coming weeks, every time we separated the two corpses, we would find them once again together, with Mr. Cooke being held down by Mr. Jacobs. They never moved;

that is, no one ever saw them move, but it scared my staff to the point where a few people had to take time off.

They were buried separately, but after a few days I got a report that Mr. Cooke's grave had been vandalised. The earth around it had been disrupted, kicked up it seemed, from underneath.

And although no one was officially found guilty of the crime, we all knew who it was, Mr. Jacobs, making sure Mr. Cooke stayed where we had put him.

In Flooded Cemeteries throughout the State

by

Karla Linn Merrifield

I saw them just the other day,
somberly clothed, veiled, emerging
as if from small houses on dirt roads,
the invisible women of Louisiana's grieving.

I touched them until my fingertips
smelled of shrimp and perspiration, breathed
oil fields and cane fields, the rice paddies
between the human legs of Louisiana in grief.

But when I voiced their myriad desires
in Cajun-Irish, pidgin English, Creole, they disappeared
as free spirits of the bayous into cypress mists,
no more the nameless mothers of Louisiana grieved.

Missing Since Tuesday

by

Ryan Howse

Morty looked out the window as Sam drove slowly through the deserted, starlit street. Sam stopped at a red light and waited for no one. Morty paused with him.

"Do you really need to obey the lights? There's nobody around."

"It's still the law," Sam said, signaling a turn.

Morty scoffed. "It's so dark out that you'd see a cop car three miles away."

"You just want a back-up story in case we don't find anything," Sam said, wiping his hand across his vision, "I can see it now in giant capital letters: 'Local public servant flagrantly ignores traffic laws.'"

"Oh, yeah, I'm sure Jason would be all over that. I'd get a big promotion, exposing the seedy underbelly of the three A.M. driving scene."

"Make sure you remember me when the print media groupies start taking up all your free time."

Sam slowed as they approached a wrought iron gate, bound with a heavy-duty chain and padlock. He stopped the car and looked at Morty.

"You know, we can still just forget about this."

"What? Why would we do that?" Morty asked.

"We're not gonna find anything. There was nothing here when I left today and there's nothing here now."

"You don't know that for sure. Six people are missing, Sam. There's got to be some trace of them."

Sam sighed and got out of the car with an electric lantern. Morty eagerly followed, bringing his notepad and camera with him. Sam put the lantern handle in his mouth and unlocked the gate. He yanked the chain free and wrapped it around his wrist before pulling the stiff metal doors apart.

"You didn't used to have to lock this, did you?" Morty said, jotting notes down.

"No, just since the disappearances." Sam all but pulled Morty inside the gate and closed it again. "I hope the next person goes missing around where you work."

"You think there'll be more?" Morty asked, a touch too excitedly. Sam shook his head and began down the path into the cemetery.

"C'mon, Morty, let's get this over with."

"What's with the long face?" Morty asked his friend, poking him with his pencil. "I'm sure you're not scared to be walking around in here."

"No, but that doesn't mean I wanna spend more time here than I have to. I already look after the place eight hours a day, not to mention all the friggin' holes I have to dig."

"Oh, can we see an open grave?" Morty swooned. "That would make such a great picture for the front page, you know? It'll give the story some more punch if the readers think that the missing people might be dead, without me having to say so."

"I'm gonna give *you* a punch. And yes, there's one up at the end of the path that I dug this afternoon."

The two walked along, disturbing the silence with their hushed speech. Only the slight rustle of grass in the wind did anything to add life to the dark. The weak glow of the cheap lantern Sam held shone like fire against the void, and illuminated the dirt path. Morty looked up, and scarcely saw the moon break through the canopy that covered the graveyard like a cold, leafy blanket.

"What are you expecting to find, anyway?" Sam asked, shining the light directly in Morty's face. Morty shielded his eyes and knocked the lantern back to where it had been.

"I don't know – anything, really. It's not like I'm looking for evidence, like DNA or whatever. I just want something that I can report on that might link the cemetery to the disappearances."

"It's already linked. Everyone knows that those people were last seen around here."

"Yeah, but those are just rumors. There hasn't been any actual news source with proof of any kind. Believe me, I checked. I'm gonna get this first."

A moment passed as Morty wrote more down into his notepad. Sam stopped walking. Morty stopped as well, after finishing his thought.

"So, what are you going to do if you find something big?" Sam asked. "Do you really want to get caught up in something like this? I've already been down to the station four times to answer questions. If you find something that proves there are bodies here, you're going to be hounded by the cops until the case is solved."

"Well, we *know* there's bodies here," Morty said, knocking a gravestone with his shoe.

"That's not what I meant, smart-ass," Sam said, catching up to Morty. "And don't kick the graves. People pay to keep those in good condition, you know."

The two continued along, nearing the end of the path. Morty looked over at his friend, obviously concerned for his well-being.

"Look, I know. I thought about all that, but…" Morty paused, for once at a loss for words. "I don't know. I'd like to actually help, if I can. Every time anything happens, I'm always there, sure, but I can't ever do anything about it. All I can do is watch and write down what happens while better people fix the problem. You know how many houses I've watched burn down through the lens of a camera while people cry on the curb? And that's a good day, because that footage is valuable to me. Just once I'd like to be the guy who fixes the problem." Sam didn't say anything as Morty finished. "I guess that probably sounds pretty stupid."

"Nah, not stupid. To tell you the truth, I figured you'd say something like that. Afraid you would. Anyway, here we are."

Sam stopped and pointed to a hole at the end of the path, dug five feet deep and seven feet long. Sam picked up a shovel stuck in a mound of displaced dirt and fiddled with the ground. Morty looked into the hole, an endless chasm in the pitch black night.

"There's no headstone. Who's the grave for?"

"Nobody."

"Nobod-"

Morty was cut short as the cold steel shovel smacked into the back of his head. He crumpled to the ground and fell with a thud down into the open grave. The tiny lantern light warped around in Morty's eyes, wrapping around the figure of Sam standing in front of it with the shovel in hand. The figure moved, and a numb thump hit Morty in the side of the face. He sputtered in pain and confusion as more dirt landed around his mouth. He tried to move, but his body refused to obey as warmth enveloped his head and neck; a chill permeated everywhere else.

"Sorry, buddy," Sam said as he buried Morty alive, "I really didn't want it to come to this."

A whistled song disturbs my sleep. Just outside the churchyard, I lie, warm and drowsy, buried within the earth, roofed by a grove of dark pines whose fallen needles and verdant mosses quilt my bed. Loath to leave a lovely pleasure, I rouse slowly, lift my head, look above to find stars twinkling through rising storm clouds. No moon. Not yet. Except for the whistle, the world seems as drowsy as I am. The ditty stops then starts again.

Fully awake now, I gaze into the night. A lone man travels, treading the hallowed ground of the cemetery that surrounds the dark-as-death stone church standing guard. The only light is the flickering gold of his lantern. Illuminated gravestones rise and waver like wraiths. Carved crosses lift their arms to fly ghostlike above the turf. The man staggers, trips over his own crapulous feet, rises. The whistling stops again. Under his breath he mutters a prayer as he peers into the murky dark beyond his light before continuing down the narrow rocky path. His lamp recedes. Marble slabs retreat into gloom. Crucifixes take roost after their flight. Through the black wrought-iron gate he passes, leaving the consecrated churchyard for the profane road that snakes from village to church to farm, resuming his warble to maintain his courage.

Had he been silent, the man might have escaped. My Master will soon awaken with the noise. Like me, he seems unwilling to disturb his repose, takes too long to stir. The whistler walks safely on. I follow his progress by his occasional hiccough, more frequent curse, as he stumbles on the wagon ruts in the road.

A nimbused blue moon rises, gilding the scalloped edges of storm clouds sliding slowly past its face.

My Master stirs. His hand strokes my withers as he growls, "Art ye ready, Morrigan?" He savors my name, rolling it over his tongue. "Mor-r-r-igan, my sweet."

Eager, I bow my assent. He touches me, my Lord Ewen, with the hand of a lover. My muscles quiver at the intimacy of his caress on my flank. I nuzzle under his arm, waiting a further sign of his affection, waiting to serve, waiting to submit.

At a delicate flick of his whip, I burst from the earth in a billowing grey mist. My nostrils flare in excitement; my hot breath steams the gelid air. Next to me, amidst a tenebrous cloud, a swirl of pitch-black announces my Lord's resurrection. He whirls his long cloak about him, swathing himself in a shroud of black-watch plaid eyes glowing fever-red. I prance before him, paw the soft ground with great hooves, nicker softly. Again, he touches me. I tremble, anticipating his need. When at last he mounts, his strong thighs embrace me.

We start slowly. He yawns. I stretch my legs. The carpet of the forest floor cushions my steps. Water oozes from the damp leafy loam muffling the noise of my hooves. My Master guides me to a gentle stream. Beneath an immense black oak tree I dabble my feet as I drink, watching wavering reflections of stars within the ripples of the dark sweet water. My soft splashes are the only sound in the silent forest beyond the eerie hoot of the night owl and the fading too-cheerful whistle of the now-distant man. His melody falters a moment, then resumes, a wee bit louder.

"We have time, Morrigan. Drink as you wish."

When I've had my fill, my Lord stretches over my head, strokes me, reassures me he is mine as much as I am his. Soft and sweet his hand follows the angle of my jaw to cup my nostrils. I breathe his scent, whinny my desire.

Another flick of the whip, harder, more urgent.

"Now, Morrigan! Fly!" His heels dig into my sides.

The night is brisk, perfect for running. To please him, I reach my long legs wide, galloping with joy, mane and tail whipping the air, streaming steamy breath behind. The weather has warmed. Whilst almost gone from the road, the snow yet lingers patchy in the fields, the stubble of harvested wheat like a day's growth of a man's beard. The way stretches miles before me, deep ruts filled with melted snow, each puddle reflecting the golden face of the moon. I bound through every one, splashing, shattering the fulvous orbs. Droplets fall to earth, yellow tears falling from the heavenly countenance. We are nearly upon the whistler. Lord Ewen laughs, low and deep, thrilling me.

The man hears, whirls, sees us. His face whitens in the lantern glow. He screams, a terrible shriek that sears my ears, then drops to his knees whimpering like a wounded animal. I race toward him at full gallop. At last he comes enough to his senses to rise and run on legs powered by fear.

I neigh in triumph, delighting in the pursuit. The game is not yet won. My Master reins me in, extending the chase, prolonging our pleasure. The man careens toward the span that crosses the creek believing evil spirits and ghosts cannot cross running water and, with a flash of fire and brimstone, my Master and I will vanish.

Just before obtaining the bridge, the man stumbles. The lantern falls, wobbling at his feet, creating a jittery play of light and shadows on nearby trees. In an instant, I am upon him, rearing high, front legs flailing the air, braying the trumpet call of death. Terrified, he flounders beneath me, feeling my hell-breath, crawling crablike to escape my hooves. Nor stripling nor full man, he has the broad back and burly thighs of a plowboy, a comely face round and smooth, lustful lips red with kisses stolen from a barmaid.

My Master's curved sword, as bright the smile as he once wore, sings out, slicing the man's head from his shoulders. A spray of dense dark blood cloaks us in sweet-smelling drops.

He shudders, my Master, then slumps over my head, moans deep and visceral in my ear.

Beneath him, I shiver.

"Steady, girl." His voice is soft, thick, sated. The fingers of one hand weave through my mane while the other strokes my neck gently, absently. My Lord yet breathes hard.

At last, he leaps from my back to stand tall beside me, his long legs white as a woman's beneath his tartan kilt. His hands rise, grasping his neck. With a twist, he plucks from his shoulders his old head, tossing it away. In the soft lantern glow shines the face of an ancient man whose once-rheumy eyes are now dry and lifeless. An empty skull with tattered glaucous hair, strips of rotting muscle parting from bone, slack jaw clacking against upper teeth, spins chin over pate before disappearing into the night. My Master, holding the lad's head before him, finds his own headless image reflected its eyes. Howling in despair, he crowns himself with this new cranium.

Centuries ago, when the King's man severed Lord Ewen's head in battle, it rolled, queued red hair, full moist lips soft and pink, surprised meadow-green eyes, on the hallowed ground of the churchyard where he, who kept pagan ways, could not retrieve it. Now and through eternity, we rise with every blue moon to search for the perfect head. Tonight with glossy brown curls gleaming in the lantern light and mossy eyes sparkling in a young man's handsome face, my Master kisses me with still-warm lips and whiskey-ed breath. "Better'n the last one, Morrigan, but 'tis na right quite yet. 'Twill do for now."

Down the dark road, regarded only by the fierce yellowed eyes of forest beasts, we gallop rapturously, escaping for the moment the prison of our fate. In savage battles my Master slashes pumpkins in the fields and whacks low-lying branches with his sword, repaying enemy soldiers for his death. When the vermilion fingers of dawn like fires of hell streak the cloudless eastern sky; my Master sighs, sheaths his weapon, tightens my reins, slows me, wheels me toward our grave.

    Storm clouds break open above us as we fly to the west, outrunning daybreak. Hard rains wash away the blood, cleanse us, baptize us. In the distance, the village cocks crow. When we reach the pines that serve as our gravestone, we return to our earthen bed, sinking slowly beneath its warm quilt of pine needles and mosses, roofed by fragrant boughs. Wrapped in his plaid shawl, we lie together spooned close like lovers. He kisses me, falls asleep with his fingers still entwined in my mane. For a moment, things are as they were before my Master fell, before I died of grief.

Phone Call from the Mausoleum

by

Jill Hand

The phone is ringing on the wall of the office of Maple Hill Cemetery. It shouldn't be ringing, but it is.

Meredith Welbeck, part-time administrative assistant, stares at the insistently ringing telephone – the one that shouldn't be ringing, but somehow, horribly, is. Her mouth hangs open and her eyes are practically popping out of her head. Meredith is normally a pretty girl, whose skin has a healthy glow, but now her skin is pasty white and her lips have lost their color.

Riiiing! goes the phone again, as if saying, *I know somebody's there. Answer me!* Meredith gets up and goes to answer it.

The phone was one of a pair that had been installed in 1956, when George Ralston Harmon III died and was entombed in the Harmon family mausoleum. The mausoleum had four granite columns in front and was built into the side of a hill. Beneath a pediment on which HARMON was inscribed in block letters was a pair of sculpted bronze doors, each weighing three hundred pounds.

Truth be told, George Harmon had been kind of a nut. He was convinced that the Russians had planted listening devices all over his house and that President Eisenhower had been kidnapped by aliens from outer space and replaced by a robot double. He was also terribly afraid of being entombed alive. He refused to be embalmed because he didn't want the undertaker to see him naked; a fear shared by a greater percentage of the population than you might think.

George's fear of being seen naked was nothing to his fear of being put into the mausoleum while still alive. It became an obsession with him. His way of dealing with it when his doctor gave him the bad news that his liver was failing was to have a telephone line installed connecting the mausoleum to the cemetery office. If he were to wake up inside his coffin, all he'd have to do was push up the lid, climb out, make his way over to the marble-topped table where a black, Western Electric Model 500 telephone sat, and lift the receiver. He wouldn't even have to dial. The phone on the wall in the office would ring automatically, alerting whoever was there to come and let him out.

The Harmons paid to keep the phone line active, year after year, decade after decade, for almost sixty years. It had never rung in all those years, not that anyone expected it to. Meredith's boss had pointed out the phone on the wall in the office on her first day and told her the story behind it.

"He stipulated in his will that the phone never be disconnected. Pick up the receiver and listen," Mrs. Duncan told Meredith.

Meredith gingerly picked it up. She heard a dial tone. She didn't like to think of the phone on the other end, covered with dust and cobwebs and surrounded by coffins containing dead bodies. It was creepy.

It was even creepier now that it was ringing. The ring sounded old-fashioned, not like the chiming sound that her cell phone made, or the *burr-burr* of the landline on her desk in the cemetery office but an insistent *brrriiing!* It sounded like telephones did in old-time TV shows from the nineteen-fifties like *The Honeymooners* and *I Love Lucy*.

Meredith cautiously walked over and picked up the receiver. A muffled male voice on the other end spoke. It said, "Lemme out!"

Meredith felt her heart give a lurch. She whispered, "Who is this?"

"Iss Shorsh. Shorsh Armo. Lemme out!" the voice croaked. The words were slurred, as if whoever was speaking wasn't used to forming words or (horrible thought!) because his lips and vocal cords had rotted. Could there be anything left of George Harmon after almost sixty years? Wouldn't he be just a skeleton by now? A skeleton that had somehow come back to life inside its tomb and was demanding to be let out? "Oh my god!" Meredith said, and sank down on the floor, the receiver clutched in her hand.

If Meredith was having a rough day, what with getting a phone call from a man who'd been dead since before Sputnik was launched,

George Arnold's day had been even worse. First, he'd had a root canal. It had hurt like hell, despite his mother assuring him it wouldn't be so bad, probably no worse than a filling. She was wrong. It had been far worse than a filling. The pain was so bad that George had cried, something that he hadn't even done when he broke his thumb while skateboarding.

The dentist had given him a parting gift of a toothbrush and a container of dental floss. George privately vowed to practice better dental hygiene. He never wanted to have another root canal if he could possibly avoid it. The dentist had also given him a prescription for six Vicodin tablets. George's mother drove him to the drugstore to get the prescription filled and then back home, where he changed into his work clothes. Over her protests, George insisted on going to work. He didn't feel bad now that he was out of the dental chair and away from the clutches of Dr. Edwin Fox, D.D.S. If his tooth started to hurt, he'd take a pill.

"If you say so," his mother said doubtfully. "I'll drive you to work. I don't want you driving if you're on pain medication. Call me when you're done and I'll come get you."

"Okay," George said.

"I love you," his mother said.

"Okay," George replied brusquely. He loved his mother very much, but he felt uncomfortable telling her so.

George was nineteen. Like Meredith, he worked at Maple Hill Cemetery, although the two of them had never met. His mother dropped him off at the groundskeeper's garage and drove away. George got out the Mighty Mow, the largest rider mower, and started mowing the grass at the back of the cemetery. When his tooth gave a twinge and started to throb he swallowed one of the pills with some Gatorade. It was still throbbing fifteen minutes later, so he popped another pill and directed the mower toward the area where the mausoleums were.

George was unfamiliar with narcotics. He was a straight arrow who, aside from sneaking an occasional beer with his buddies, never touched alcohol and never did drugs. He therefore ascribed the happy feeling that washed over him like a soft, pleasant wave as coming from it being a fine, sunny day, and from driving the Mighty Mow, something he enjoyed doing immensely but the head groundskeeper rarely let him do. The head groundskeeper was away on vacation so George had seized the opportunity to indulge himself.

He also supposed he felt happy because he was alive whereas the people buried in the cemetery were dead. He felt so elated by this state of affairs that he started to sing.

"I'm alive and you're not," he sang to the headstone of Louis Epsom Phelps (1874-1943) Greatly Missed By All Who Knew Him. Really belting it out, he sang, "You're worm food, loser, but I'm aliiiiive! I win and you lose hahaha!"

Fortunately, the Mighty Mow's engine was noisy, so nobody would have been able to hear what George was singing, not that there was anyone around to hear it. That part of the cemetery was deserted.

The Mighty Mow was slowly moving up the side of the hill that encased the Harmon mausoleum. If the head groundskeeper had been there he would have shouted to George to stop. The ground at the top of the hill was unstable. It might not bear the mower's seven hundred and fifty-pound weight, not to mention George's one hundred and eighty-five pounds. The groundskeepers were supposed to use one of the smaller, hand-pushed mowers when attending to the grass on top of the Harmon mausoleum, but George was feeling so happy that he had forgotten.

Then disaster struck. One moment George was seated atop the Mighty Mow, high as a kite, happily singing a song from his childhood about a cartoon character named Benny the Big Blue Hippo who enjoys eating pizza and reciting the alphabet, and the next he was falling.

You see, the builders of the Harmon mausoleum had a dirty little secret. While all the visible parts of the structure were solidly constructed of the highest quality Vermont granite, the roof was made of a thin layer of poured concrete. The builders had deliberately shortchanged the Harmons when the mausoleum was installed back in 1918. Nobody was any the wiser until the moment the old concrete shattered like ice breaking up on a pond, sending George plunging through the roof, still atop the Mighty Mow.

"Awf!" he cried in surprise. Then his head struck the granite floor and he passed out.

Meredith was still sitting on the floor of the office holding onto the telephone receiver when her boss, Helen Duncan came in, accompanied by an old couple named Ted and Evelyn Ulrich. The Ulrichs were in their late eighties and had grudgingly come around to accepting the idea that they might die someday. They'd been to visit the crypt, where they were thinking of purchasing three spaces: two for themselves and one for Evelyn's mother.

Evelyn's mother, who had been a terror when she was alive, was currently interred in a plot in a part of the cemetery called Peaceful Haven. Evelyn had been horrified to find a partially smoked marijuana cigarette on her mother's grave. To her way of thinking, that meant Peaceful Haven had become a bad neighborhood. Evelyn felt it was her duty to get her mother out of there and into a better neighborhood, possibly somewhere in the middle tier of the crypt's upscale Garden of Eternal Repose.

"It's expensive," Ted was saying as the trio walked into the office. "It's going to cost a lot of money and we said we were going to pay for Mason's college." Mason was their youngest granddaughter.

Evelyn replied that her first duty was to her mother. "I couldn't live with myself if I found a you-know-what on her grave."

Helen asked, "What's a you-know-what?"

"A thingy," Evelyn whispered.

It took Helen a few seconds to catch on. It was the embarrassed expression on Ted's face that did it. "Do you mean a condom?" she asked.

Evelyn was spared from answering by catching sight of Meredith sitting on the floor. "What's the matter? Are you ill?' Noticing the telephone receiver in Meredith's hand, she asked, "Did someone call with bad news?"

"Hey," said Ted interestedly. He shuffled over to where Meredith sat, his deck shoes making squeaking noises on the linoleum floor, and leaned down to look. "Isn't that the phone that's connected to the mausoleum?"

The phone was famous in local lore. The weekly newspaper had even done a piece about it.

Meredith turned a stricken face to Helen. "He called," she said.

"Who did?" Helen asked. Her hip was hurting and she eased herself into a chair. "Who called?"

"George Harmon. He said to let him out."

"Nonsense," said Ted. "It's just some kid fooling around. He's probably hooked up to a computer somewhere, doing hacking." Ted's knowledge of how computers worked was hazy at best. He took the receiver from Meredith's hand and spoke sternly into it. "You frightened a young girl, you hooligan! Hang up right now, or I'm calling the police!"

A voice spoke back, "Elp! Get ee out. I'm in uh aussoleum."

Ted had seen combat in Korea. He considered himself to be pretty tough, but the mushy, croaking voice was unsettling. Equally unsettling was Evelyn's reaction. She'd fallen to her knees and cast her eyes up to the ceiling, her hands clasped in prayer.

"On the day of judgement, the dead shall rise and the wicked shall be punished. So the Bible tells us," she crowed. "Judgement Day has arrived! Praise God! Thank you, Lord Jesus, for returning to smite the evil-doers."

Evelyn had fallen in with a group of evangelicals who had erected an enormous megachurch on the outskirts of town. The preacher liked to dwell on the terrible punishments that would be meted out to sinners when Jesus returned. Evelyn would smile, imagining her daughters-in-law, all of whom she detested, being on the receiving end of those punishments.

Ted, who didn't share his wife's religious mania, sternly told her to look out the window. "Do you see any graves opening up and dead people climbing out? I don't. That means it's not Judgement Day, so calm down, for Christ's sake."

"Don't take the Lord's name in vain," Evelyn snapped. "They might not all be rising at the same time. Maybe Mister Harmon is the first to rise."

Ted doubted it. "For Chri… I mean for Pete's sake, he hasn't risen from the dead. It's probably just kids. They broke into the mausoleum and they're fooling around in there." He felt a return of his old warrior spirit. Settling his tweed driving cap firmly on his head he announced, "I'm going to go catch the little bastards in the act."

"Shouldn't we get Milt to go?" Meredith asked. Milt was the cemetery's security guard.

Helen said Milt wasn't around. He'd called in saying he'd had a family emergency. Milt frequently had family emergencies. This latest one had taken him to the Tally-Ho

Tavern, where he was ensconced on a bar stool, drinking boilermakers and watching two women argue profanely over ownership of a dog on *Judge Judy*.

Helen got the keys to the mausoleum out of her desk and hoisted herself out of her seat. Gripping the handles of her walker, she said, "Let's go take a look."

The first person to be entombed in the Harmon mausoleum was Edward Forrestal Harmon (1900–1918.) Edward was a promising youth who'd left Princeton and gone off to fight in World War I. He returned from the war without a scratch on him, only to die shortly afterwards in the influenza pandemic. The mausoleum had been constructed in readiness for his grandfather, Senator Abner Hastings Harmon, who everyone thought was on his last legs. To his family's surprise (and not a little disappointment) Abner went on to live another twenty years, rejuvenated by his marriage to a twenty-year-old who worked in a candy shop on the boardwalk in Atlantic City.

Edward, unlike his cousin George, had been embalmed. Unfortunately, so many people were dying in the pandemic that undertakers ran short of embalming fluid. They were feverishly working overtime preparing bodies for burial to the point that some of them were given a rush job. Edward, who'd been a handsome fellow who resembled the young F. Scott Fitzgerald, had been among those who'd been hastily clapped into their coffins without proper embalming. As a consequence, when the Mighty Mow fell into the mausoleum with a tremendous crash, he no longer looked like the dashing young chronicler of the Jazz Age escapades of flaming youth. The Mighty Mow slammed into the shelf where Edward's coffin lay, disgorging him and causing him to tumble out and roll across the floor, where he came to rest face-to-face with the unconscious George Arnold.

George liked horror movies, the more gruesome the better. He'd enjoyed such classics as *Hell Harvest I, II and III* and *Pledge Week Massacre.* You'd think he'd be delighted to wake up staring into the eyes of the late Edward Harmon but such was not the case. Not that Edward had eyes anymore, exactly, they were more like dried up pieces of chewing gum that had fallen back into his skull. His once-handsome nose was gone, leaving two slits. His lips had popped their stitches and drawn back, revealing a broad grin. Edward was still wearing his olive green doughboy uniform, which was in better condition than the rest of him.

George scrambled to his feet. He'd bitten his tongue when his head hit the floor and his mouth was filled with blood. "Oh, shit! Oh, shit!" he cried, only it came out as "aw, shee!" He knew where he was. He was inside the big mausoleum that was set into the hillside. The place was in ruins. The Mighty Mow had broken the granite shelf where Edward Harmon had formerly reposed and bits of his coffin and its stained satin lining were scattered on the floor, along with chunks of concrete from the roof and clods of dirt. George didn't want to look at the thing that lay sprawled on the floor, its skinny legs wrapped in puttees. The Mighty Mow was all bashed up and the granite floor was cracked. George groaned. He was going to be in big trouble. He'd sprained his ankle and a lump was rising on his head where he'd cracked it against the floor.

"Aw, shee!" he moaned.

The thing to do was to get out, quickly. But how? Favoring his ankle, George hopped over on one foot and tried the heavy, bronze doors, finding them locked. The hole in the ceiling offered another avenue of escape, but it was too high for him to reach. He knew! He'd call for help. He reached into his pocket for his cell phone only to realize that he'd left it in his room when he'd changed into his work clothes. "Aw, shee!" he said again, despairingly. Then his desperate gaze caught sight of the table that held an old-fashioned, black telephone covered with a thick fur of dust. He remembered Rudy Bassett, the head groundskeeper, telling him about there being a phone in one of the mausoleums that was put in by some rich guy who was afraid of being entombed alive. This had to be it. Now if only it were still connected...

"Oh, please, oh, please," he whispered as he hopped over to the table and lifted the receiver. Yes! It was ringing. The ringing stopped as someone on the other end answered.

"Lemme out!" he said.

Ted Ulrich strode manfully toward his car, a black, 2001 Cadillac Coup de Ville the size of a small yacht. He was followed by Evelyn, who was fussily buttoning her sweater. Helen Duncan and Meredith took up the rear. They got in and headed toward the rear of the cemetery where the mausoleum was. The speed limit on the cemetery roadways was 20 mph, but Ted was doing forty in his haste to lay his hands on the pranksters.

He pulled up in front of the mausoleum, got out, and took a look around. The sculpted bronze doors were shut and there was no sign of anyone, but then a shadowy form loomed behind the thick glass that backed the doors. It waved its arms frantically and pounded on the glass, emitting muffled cries. Its hair was standing on end and blood dripped down its chin.

"Ugh, ugh!" it cried.

"What the hell?" Ted yelped, taking a step backward.

"It's a zombie!" gasped Meredith. It would get Ted first, and then it would force its way into the car where she and Helen and Evelyn sat, gaping in shock at the shambling figure visible behind the glass. Ted had taken the keys with him or she'd have driven away. Oh, why had she been foolish enough to take a job in a cemetery?

"That's not a zombie," said Helen. "It's one of the groundskeepers. George-something. He must have gotten locked in, goodness knows how."

She unlocked the door to the mausoleum and George Arnold stumbled out. Helen surveyed the mess inside and shook her head. They'd have to notify the insurance company and call a funeral home to come and do something about the corpse on the floor. They'd need to call the Harmons, too. Helen wasn't looking forward to it, but it had to be done.

"Listen," George said hopefully. "I think maybe I might have undergone severe psychological trauma in there so maybe…"

Helen's steely gaze stopped him before he could finish what he was about to say, which was that maybe he was entitled to a substantial sum of money as recompense.

"Or maybe not," he said meekly.

And that was that. The mausoleum was repaired. Upon Rudy Bassett's return, George was fired for his escapade with the Mighty Mow. He enrolled in community college, where he wrote a wildly exaggerated account for the student newspaper about his experience in the mausoleum entitled "Trapped Among the Dead!" It made him something of a campus hero.

George Harmon rests peacefully in his replacement coffin inside the repaired mausoleum. The phone line remains connected, just in case.

Pine Grove Cemetery

by

Skye Winters

The pang hit the fine lining of Dan Kwoksi's heart with enough strength he wanted to raise a hand to cradle the very spot on his chest, yet the wind had him holding down the contract, ready to sign. He could have taken this small pain as an omen to his final event, yet he was a man of greater simplicity and believed life was merely life, omens being a thing of stories.

"The grave markers will be removed by the end of the day," he told the buyer. They shook hands, Kwoski's hand was shaky by now and he attributed his sudden imbalance to excitement. He'd just made $50,000. He leaned against his shiny black car, saluting the buyer farewell then scanned the graveyard, not seeing the head stones nor bumps in the earth, but instead, the potential of the land, envisioning what it would become.

It was the oldest graveyard on the island, the graves dated back to the 1800s. The privately owned land had been passed down to him from a long line of relatives, none of whom were alive. Teenagers partied here, raccoons took up home in the surrounding trees. Groundkeepers had been hired only a few times a year when heritage tours were organized, even then, the pay was nothing compared to this. He couldn't think of a reason *not* to sell the land, as the boxed up corpses were surely disintegrated. He tried to envision the past when this very graveyard's first grave had been dug. The same pang that reached for his heart while signing returned. This time the intensity increased, making him lose grasp of his seller's copy to clutch the spot on his chest, the coat, shirt, skin and ribs away from his heart. The important paper, his winnings as he saw it, ran away in the breeze eventually sticking to the headstone of Gerda Johnson 1805–1872. As a fine line of sweat sprung across his body, dampening his newly pressed suit that now felt like it was tightening onto his body, he saw the paper being lifted into midair. He fell to his knees while his heart squeezed one final attempt at life. He let out a groan that sounded unfamiliar and struggled to breathe. The paper crumpled into a ball by no physical source he could see and oddly the pain subsided until it was nothing. An old man stood over him and offered his hand.

"Welcome to Pine Grove Cemetery." The old man's voice crackled.

Kwoski waved the hand away and stood up on his own. "I know where I am," he whispered. He brushed the dirt from his knees and turned to his car, all the while searching for his keys within his pockets. They weren't there, and he began searching the ground where he'd collapsed, assuming they'd fallen.

The older man shook his head at Kwoski and turned to an equally older woman, who glared at him. "Now you're making friends with him? He signs our home over and now..." Her words trailed off as Kwoski stomped the ground.

"I've lost my keys," he grumbled.

"That's not all you've lost," the woman commented.

The old man took her hand. "Go easy on him, Gerda. He doesn't know yet."

As Kwoski tried in vain to retrace his steps and find his keys he found his memory fading. Had he and the buyer walked the scope of the yard or had they stayed on the drive? Something darted out from behind a taller headstone to hide behind another.

"What was that?" His heart should have picked up a beat, for the movement surprised him, yet he found himself standing placid. No physical sensation of any kind.

"It's only Juliette. She's never met anyone who has stayed this long. She's curious is all." The old man called to her, and a young girl stepped out. She wore a white night dress, her hair long with a ring of dried flowers, set like a crown upon her head. Apprehensively, she crept closer. Kwoski noticed her feet were bare. When she reached them she hid behind the older woman and peeked around at him.

"The name's Herald Johnson." The old man offered his hand. "My wife, Gerda, and this here's Juliette."

Kwoski took the old man's hand. "Nice to meet you. I'm-"

The old woman spat on the ground. "Dan Kwoski, we know." She didn't offer her hand, but pulled the small girl out from behind her, keeping her hands on her shoulders. "He's no harm," she told the girl. "He's already done the worst."

Kwoski shook his head. "I'm sorry, am I missing something? What have I done that is so wrong?" Kwoski didn't yet know he was dead, nor did he realize he'd signed over their peaceful home. Over time, when realization sunk in that he was indeed dead, he would try to leave, being trapped by a translucent wall he could never cross.

"Not until you accept it," the old man explained. Gerda nor the girl would ever pay attention to him more than they had that first day.

"Then why don't you leave?" Kwoski asked.

"We like it here. Juliette was too young to realize what happened to her and I don't have the heart to tell her. Gerda would miss her an awful lot."

Six months later, the earth had been leveled, new grass planted and a house, with no basement stood waiting for their arrivals: a family of four.

Gerda had accepted this, milling about the new kitchen as the living mother organized the cupboards and placed things on the counter. Gerda marveled over the fridge, stove and even once asked Kwoski about the microwave. She didn't agree with how the living mother set certain things up, believing the butter should sit on the counter, rather than in the fridge, shaking her head when the bread was left out and promptly placing it in the bread box.

These sorts of adjustments unnerved the living mother. "Unless the kids have suddenly started putting stuff away, I think this house is haunted," she told her husband one night when she found the kitchen table cleared, the chairs pushed in.

"Honey, *no one* else has lived here. It's a brand-new house!" He thought his wife may be losing her mind.

"Gerda, you gotta stop moving stuff," Old Herald told her time and again.

Juliette was no better with the children. She played with their toys, bringing the dolls out to the yard, creating arguments between the siblings. "He took my dolls and covered them in mud!"

The boy would yell back. "She woke me up in the middle of the night again and wrecked my block castle!"

Only once had Herald made the mistake of passing the living father the wrench he'd misplaced while working under the hood of his car. Herald had only wanted to help the man and hear the engine turn over. He'd never seen the workings of these new automobiles so closely.

"Maybe they're friendly ghosts," the living father whispered to his wife in the quiet of the living room one night. His wife wasn't sure if he was joking or not.

The four ghosts sat among them, listening intently.

"I don't like it," the living mother cried. "Let's move," she suggested.

Juliette cried. She didn't want to be alone again, now that she had discovered other children.

Kwoski had grown sullen, knowing he missed his own family he could no longer remember. It had taken time, but he realized, he was, indeed dead.

"It's time," Herald told Gerda.

"Don't be silly, Herald."

"For Juliette," he replied. He led his wife and Juliette from the house, into the front yard, Kwoski following a few steps behind.

They came to the edge of the property, and Kwoski watched as old Herald took Gerda's face in his hands and kissed her. "Let's do it again," he told her. She had tears, ghostlike in the way they didn't run in rivers, but congealed as icy lakes in the wrinkles her once living life had formed. She took Juliette's hand in her own. Old Herald turned to Kwoski.

"Let's leave this family be," he said. "Won't you join us?"

Kwoski nodded, not sure where they were going and followed the old couple with Juliette through a tear in the atmosphere. Instantly, his ghost body fell from his Spirit and he lifted off into an indescribable fluency that allowed him to move into his next life.

The living family woke the next day, their home feeling empty in a way they weren't sure if they were imagining or not.

Years later, after their kids had grown up and moved away and they too had moved on, Herald, Gerda and their daughter, Juliette reborn again, would move into the house, not knowing why the place seemed familiar, but content to be there. Kwoski drove by on his way to work each morning, always drawn to slow his car just a little to stare into the windows of the old house, not sure himself why he felt the pull.

While she walked down the deserted road,
  The woman felt a very big unnatural load;
A load that was just pulling down her spirit.
And it made her lose her characteristic wit.

For no reason at all she felt very frightened.
And her apprehensions were so heightened
When just ahead of her she saw a graveyard.
And then she stopped and was on total guard.

She stared hard at a big marble gravestone.
For on it was seated a white-dressed crone.
And the crone looked at her so very steadily
That she was just drawn to her very readily.

When she got very close to the smiling djin
She nearly jumped out of her ashen skin.
And this was because the face of the crone.
The face was exactly the same as her own.

Max watched Peggy hurrying into their booth at the "Veg-Out" restaurant in London. He smiled thinking how much she matched the restaurant with her vintage clothes and her fingerless gloves. Peggy returned his smile, sat down and reached into her bag for her book. Max held out his hand and pushed the book down on the table.

"Just a minute Peggy, can we talk?"

"Sure!"

"I mean a talk, a real talk."

"Oh, should I be scared? We agreed no serious, future talk, until after graduation."

"It's your graduation. I have another year to finance before I have my doctorate, then I can relax."

"Is that what we're talking about?"

"I'm wondering about our plans; going to Toronto, getting jobs and having fun in the city for the summer."

"That still sounds good to me."

"I've been offered a job."

"You have, where, what? When did you have time for a job interview?"

"Professor Tompkins came to me last week and asked me if I'd be interested. It includes a house and a great source of material for my doctoral thesis."

"You knew this a week ago? Why did you wait so long to tell me?" Peggy jumped up and went over to his side of the booth to hug him. "This sounds perfect. We don't have to go to Toronto. I can keep my job here. I'll have time to work out plans for my Master's degree in the fall. History is too broad a topic; I have to narrow it down."

"It isn't here."

"Where is it?"

"It's in St. Thomas. It's a feasibility study for the Unitarian church. They want someone to study the area and see if a fellowship will prosper."

"Max, that sounds a lot like being a minister to me. I told you I could never be a minister's wife. My mother was a preacher's kid; she's told me lots of stories."

"No, it's not as a minister, but it is studying a ministry for the area."

"St. Thomas? What would I do in St. Thomas?" Peggy paused, "Maybe we should spend the summer apart." Max turned quickly to look at her, "You need time to think," was her answer to his unasked question. She continued reasoning out loud, "Maybe I need time to think. This plan scares me and it is closer and closer to ministry. You said you like the inclusive premise of the Unitarians and now you're doing a study for them. What's next?" Peggy moved back to her side of the table, just as the waiter came for their order.

"Can you give us a minute?" Max asked the waiter.

"Please, Peggy, this is why I didn't tell you. I knew you would jump to conclusions." His look begged her to stay and talk.

"What do you want me to do? Go along, do whatever you want me to do? Does that sound like me?"

"No, and I wouldn't want you to be like that. But I do want you to give this idea a chance. I want you to trust me and know that you are important. If it doesn't work for you, it doesn't work for me. We are engaged, our future is together."

"I'm listening. But first we'd better order."

After they ordered Max took a deep breath. He knew what he said next would make or break their summer.

"Having two places is exhausting. I am paying for an apartment and you're paying for an apartment. We're always together, at one place or the other. Together, in one place for the summer, would be ideal."

"You mean move in together?"

"Yes, I guess I do mean that. I've already asked you to marry me and you agreed."

Peggy looked shocked. Obviously, she was not prepared for this conversation. "I see my future with you, too. I just never thought of moving in together. It seems so, so, so, so mature."

Max couldn't help it. He had to laugh.

"It's not funny Max- this is serious."

Max put on his most serious face. "Is that better?"

Peggy couldn't help but grin. She sighed a big sigh as she reached out and touched his face.

"I need to take time to think about this."

Max looked a little relieved and made a suggestion. "Let's enjoy our lunch and tomorrow we'll take a drive to St. Thomas. I'll show you the house, we'll look at the town together and then we'll have another serious talk. Deal?"

"Deal."

The next morning, Peggy picked Max up in her restored VW Beetle. "You can drive Max, you know the way. How far is St. Thomas from here?"

"Not far. Just a little over half an hour."

"What is St. Thomas famous for?"

"Well, they have an elephant."

"An elephant?"

"Well, not really an elephant. Not a live elephant. It's a statue of Jumbo, the famous circus elephant. He was killed in

St. Thomas on the railroad tracks and they have a statue as a memorial to him."

Peggy didn't say anything for a while. She just stared straight ahead. "So, we're driving to a town and all you have to say for it is that it has a dead elephant?"

"Well, it has a lot of churches but, I wasn't sure you'd want to hear about that. There are two beautiful parks and a library and a hospital and I think they even have a yarn shop."

Peggy reached into her bag and pulled out her knitting. "Now that you mention it, I think I'll knit for a while. It helps me think."

"Go ahead, it's not that far."

Max relaxed his grip on the steering wheel. He realized that thinking might just be a good idea. He wanted Peggy to go with him this summer. He knew she'd like to go to Toronto, not to be near her family, but to be near the restaurants and the theatre. Restaurants and theatre was not something his family understood.

His father wanted him to come to work on the farm, but another summer on the farm was more than he could handle. Student loans had been impossible because the farm looked like such a big asset. His dad loaned him the money and Max promised to pay it all back as soon as he graduated. It made sense to work on the farm, but his father insisted on doing everything his way and fights were inevitable.

He needed to make a break, but going to Toronto made him look as irresponsible as his father said he was. A really good job was something Max could justify. He looked over at Peggy. She did look happier knitting.

Peggy looked at Max and smiled. She loved him, she knew that for sure. Had love made her mother give up her dreams of being a biologist to follow her father? Peggy knit faster. She knew she couldn't give up her dreams. She had talent as a historian. Professor Manley told her just last week she had a gift for seeing how things might have been and making history come alive. She needed to go on with her Master's and she was starting to tie it into women's studies and the history of forgotten women. How could she give that up?

Max seems to be going into the church, the very institution that helped dominate women. She and Max had met in a women's studies course and one of the reasons she fell in love with him was because she thought he understood. That and his gorgeous smile and his strong farmer's hands and build. Peggy put her knitting down. Thinking was impossible when she thought about how much she loved Max.

"Well, we're here, I think. I see an elephant up there." Max was pointing out the window up a hill and, sure enough, there was an elephant. "Now if I can just figure out how to get there."

Max and Peggy walked around Jumbo and Max took pictures of Peggy reaching up for the tusks. "You look so tiny," Max shouted.

"Let me take your picture and see how big you look." Max laughed and took hold of the tail and pretended he was running behind Jumbo.

They found a tourist booth in the nearby railway car and it was open for business with lots of maps and information about St. Thomas. Max asked if there was anything else to do in St. Thomas, and for directions to Centre Street.

"You're only a couple of blocks from Centre Street." The tourist guide spread out a city map and pointed it out. "You're really close to the old St. Thomas Church and they have guided tours every day this summer. This whole area of St. Thomas is called a historic district and the church goes back to the early 1800s."

Max and Peggy looked at each other. "History! A historic church, you wouldn't be interested in a historical church would you?" Max teased.

"Very funny." Peggy looked at the tour guide "I'm a history major."

The tour guide knew she was on to something they would love to do. "You can leave your car here and walk if you want to. Just up the road, a little, almost across from here you'll see a street. It goes to the old railroad track, turn east and you can't miss the graveyard. One of the tour guides will give you directions to Centre Street, and you can circle back past the yarn store, and you'll be back here."

"This tiny street has a name, King Street. Imagine that. It really is a street." Max put his arms around Peggy and laughed. "I'll save you from the traffic."

"Look at these houses. They're really old. Did you see the brick work on the big house at the corner?" Peggy stood still and turned around so she could take it all in. "It's so old I can feel the people who used to live in it."

"I wonder if the house they're giving us to live in is this old." Max looked hopefully at Peggy. Would she notice that, 'us'. Would she give his plan a chance?

"Us?" Peggy raised her eyebrows with the question.

"Well, I told Professor Tompkins, that whatever I do this summer, I will have to make sure my fiancée agrees."

"Oh, you did, did you? And what did he say?"

"He said to bring her along. It's a great place to spend the summer so close to the Port Stanley beach."

"Maybe I can study the history of this place. Maybe start working on the thesis for my master's."

Max let out a cheer, grabbed her and swung her around. The big skirt on her sundress ballooned out around them.

"Put me down, you big clown. I said, maybe." She straightened her skirt and tried to hide her grin.

"I'll take 'maybe.'" Max walked to the corner. "I see the graveyard- the church must be up here."

Lots of mature trees filled the churchyard and it was surrounded by a wrought iron fence. The wind through the trees made them slow down and walk quietly under the arched entryway.

Soon they were inside the church and the guide was well into its history when he pointed to a large plaque listing the ministers who had served at the old St. Thomas Church.

Rev. Alex McIntosh, 1824–1829

Rev. E.T. Boswell, 1829

Rev. Mark Burnham, 1829–1852

Rev. A. St. George Caulfield, 1852–1873

Rev. Stephen B. Kellogg 1874–1875

Rev. T. Des Barres 1876–1877.

"What about their wives? Do you have a record of them?" asked Peggy.

"I'm not sure, I've never seen a list, but some are buried here," responded the guide. "Mrs. Berham and Maria Baldwin but Maria's husband was not exactly a minister here."

Peggy was obviously concerned. "So the rest are all forgotten?"

"I'm not sure, but I can see what I can find out, I have some books here and the library has a good history section. There's also a lot of information at the local archives."

Peggy was quiet for the rest of the tour. When they moved outside, the tour guide pointed out Burnham's wife's grave. Peggy knelt down beside it and brushed off the grass and dirt so she could read the inscription. "Look here," she said, pointing to some smaller words. "It says 'she was a kind and generous woman', I wonder who wrote that. She died years after her husband."

They walked through the gravestones and heard more stories about the black gravesite known as the witch's grave. "Who was she married to?" Peggy wondered aloud.

"Rev. M. S. Baldwin was a travelling curate. She was Maria Ermatinger and she lived here in St. Thomas with her parents until she married Rev. Baldwin. I think they were in Port Dover parish where Rev. Baldwin was serving when she died in childbirth, she was only nineteen. Her father was very wealthy and he brought the white gravestone and markers from Toronto. The acid in the rain turned the limestone black. There is often a stray black cat around and that makes for lots of ghost stories and folk legends." After more stories and more legends about the graves, the tour guide asked Max and Peggy if they had any questions.

"Can you tell me where 56 Centre Street is?" asked Max.

"Oh, I see why you were so interested in the ministers."

"What do you mean?"

"56 Centre Street was where Rev. Burnham lived."

Max stared at the guide, "We didn't know that."

"You didn't?"

"No, but we have a chance to live there for the summer." Max looked at Peggy and could see she was tired and hot. "I think maybe we should go for lunch."

"I'll find all the information we have about the Burnham's and have it ready for you if you come back." The guide looked at Max, then at Peggy and recommended they go for lunch at the corner cafe.

Peggy looked relieved. "Thanks, I'm hungry- the closer the food is the better."

"We have to meet at the house at two—it's almost one o'clock, so we'll come back after that." Max grabbed Peggy's hand and they were off.

Peggy talked all through lunch about the ministers' wives and the fact that their history was forgotten. Max reminded her that they were not actual employees of the church so maybe that was why they weren't mentioned. He was relieved when the time came to go. He didn't need to get into an argument he knew he would lose.

"Let's go see if this house is fit to live in," Max said with some relief. "Look, you can see the elephant from here. We've only been a few blocks away all morning."

"I feel like I've been to another world and back. Isn't history the best Max?"

"If it gets you to stay with me in St. Thomas for the summer, I'll love it forever."

"Ahhh Max, you don't get it. You just don't get it."

"But I get you, Peggy. That's the main thing."

"I haven't made up my mind yet, Max. How do I even begin to find out about these forgotten women? Who really cares? Who writes their history? That's what I'm interested in!"

"There's still a history section at the public library and archives to check out. Don't give up on St Thomas yet."

"I won't. Oh look, there's 56 Centre Street. It looks like all the other houses around here."

"Here's Mr. Carter now, that's the real estate person Professor Tompkins said would meet us." Max put one arm around Peggy and shook Mr. Carter's hand. "I'm Max and this is my fianceé, Peggy."

"Call me John. I'm pleased to meet you both. I haven't been in the house since the tenants left so I hope it is cleaned up. We'll find out together."

Max and Peggy remarked about the rooms' high ceilings and the large windows. They helped open the windows as they went from room to room and put in the screens that were propped up below them. The air changed and soon as they had a cross breeze.

John pointed out that this was an old building. "Some of the houses here have been designated as heritage homes and they are actually not as old as this one. You can see where the newer parts were upgraded for the kitchen and bathroom so they could have electricity and plumbing. There's some furniture in the basement that has been saved from the original owners. I think it was a manse then. We can't decide what to do with it."

"Can I see it?" Peggy asked.

"Well, it's in the basement, which is in disrepair. I'm not sure if there is even light."

John went over to the basement door and reached for a light switch, "Yes, there is light. You're welcome to look, but be careful."

Max looked doubtful. "Are you sure? I'll look around outside and be right back."

"Okay, I'll be fine." Peggy heard Max mumble about her being a history major and crazy about the old stuff.

Peggy looked around the basement until her eyes adjusted and she found an old bed frame leaning up against a vanity table with mirrors.

"How did this vanity ever survive?" she wondered. She repositioned the frame and could see it had a center drawer and two side drawers, a center mirror and two side mirrors.

"Wow, this is old," thought Peggy.

She brushed off some dust and could see that the wood was oak and the mirrors were the old beveled kind. There was a dusty trunk nearby and she pulled it over so she could sit in front of the vanity. In her imagination, she saw it polished with lemon oil. She imagined putting some of the fancy linen doilies she'd seen while shopping in vintage shops in each section under the mirrors. She brushed at the mirrors trying to see if there was damage- there was a shadow that couldn't be cleared away. Peggy took a deep breath and rested her hand on the vanity. She could almost feel the hair brush that was not there. She could see it moving up to brush the hair of the woman in the shadow.

"Thank you, Peggy."

"For what?" whispered Peggy.

"For telling our story."

"I haven't told your story yet have I?"

"I'm Mark Burnham's wife. My real name is Mehitabel, but friends call me Hetty. The word we hear on this side is that you are going to tell the story of forgotten ministers' wives and we have some really good stories to tell."

"We?" Peggy managed to squeak out.

"There are lots of us and your grandmother even asked if she could help. She isn't from around here but she seems sure she can help. You can do this Peggy, and we are all going to help you."

"Thanks, I think."

"You're welcome."

The shadow cleared and Peggy saw the mirror was in perfect condition.

"Peggy? Are you still down there?" Max yelled down the stairs

"Yes. I found a beautiful vanity."

"Can you come up, Mr. Carter has to leave and he wants to know if we want the place for the summer."

Peggy hurried up the stairs remembering to duck where the main floor joined the foundation. Max looked at her as she brushed dust and spider webs off her dress.

"Are you all right? You look pale."

"I'm fine."

"We can decide today or we can have another week if we need it, then they will have to put it on the market."

"Can we use the furniture in the basement?" Peggy asked.

"Of course, I can't see any reason why not. It would be good to get it cleaned up and decide what to do with it." John shrugged and turned to look at Max.

"Then, I definitely want to stay," said Peggy.

Max was wide-eyed with surprise. Mr. Carter shook his head.

"Well you heard the lady; it's yours for the summer. Thank you, Max. And thank you, Peggy." John held his hand out to Max.

"Thank you, Mr. Carter, thank you very much." Max shook his hand a little harder than he needed to.

It will all end soon enough
you'll be dead and leave your stuff
These once treasured things
sentimental collectables
comic books, baseball cards
odd coins, stamps, art
old books, photo and
record albums, letters
antiques, drawings . . .
that bust of Augustus Caesar
those teak wood Buddha's
one stuffed armadillo . . .
a framed portrait of my grandmother, who I never met
that my grandchildren will likely toss away with the rest

These inherited heirlooms and assorted goods
you will release as you lose your final breath
writhing perhaps on yellow linoleum
or upon that handwoven Chinese rug

Those with first dibs collect their keepsakes
as most is dispensed, dispersed—a diaspora of stuff
frittered away like dandelion fluff, on into thrift stores,
bins and aisles teeming with other dead-people-things
packed up, buried, picked over, stored, hoarded
while crows, termites, maggots, worms
our consuming cousins
fall in line

Another rosebud dud, another molecule erased
Your face lingering on after you're gone
trapped in glass and frame, in a pile perhaps
stacked high like Auschwitz eyewear, your gold teeth
melted down, sold or in the lost or found—you
rejoining the greater party—that one no one is invited to
that everyone must attend

Thou Shalt Not

by

Ann Martin

It had been a long day. First the men's breakfast, as always, on the first Saturday of the month, but then, with Angela out of action, he'd had to do the weekend shopping. He'd made his own lunch, too, then three pastoral visits, a marriage preparation session with a young couple and finally, a late afternoon funeral.

Josh Carter had been taken before his time, nobody could argue with that, except perhaps Josh's maker, who may have been quite satisfied with the day and the hour. Nevertheless, the local maintenance man and gardener had been in his prime and had liked to work with a naked torso to prove it. There had been quite a gaggle of weeping women at the funeral, but then women had been Josh's thing, that and the drink. As it turned out, it was the drink that had contributed largely to his passing.

Late last Saturday night, through the pouring rain and with his usual skinful, Josh had been riding his Harley full throttle home from the pub. He couldn't have reckoned on rocks being littered all over the wet road, but as someone once famously said, shit happens. The police thought the rain must have caused the rockslide.

It had been a long day and now it was turning into night. The winter darkness fell long before he had washed up after his solitary dinner. He was already missing Angela terribly, but that couldn't be helped. He put on his gardening jacket, collected the shovel from the shed and returned to the grave that he'd prayed over that afternoon. Even with the soil so recently turned, it took him a couple of hours to open it up. But Josh Carter hadn't been the only muscular bloke in town and at last the shovel thumped onto the lid of the coffin. Then he knew he could go and fetch Angela.

She was still slumped in the bottom of the wardrobe, still inside two heavy duty garbage bags. Her small, slender figure had been one of her most attractive attributes, but even so, she was a dead weight as he heaved her onto his shoulder. What else would she be? He smiled ironically at the pun that had flitted through his head.

He'd kept his good black shoes on the whole time, because those were the soles that would have been imprinted around the grave after the funeral anyway.

There you are then, my dear, just what you wanted. Sleeping together forever.

He heard the thud as her body hit the coffin. Then it took him another hour to shovel the earth back on top of the pair of them.

By the time he'd showered and put on his pyjamas it was almost midnight. He was so looking forward to a deep, comfortable sleep, when, *hell and damnation*, he remembered that he hadn't written tomorrow's sermon.

With a heavy sigh, he dragged on his slippers and dressing gown, trudged into his study and switched on his laptop.

This morning I continue my series of reflections upon the ten commandments. Exodus 20, verse 13: Thou shalt not kill.

The Van Arsdale Secret

by

Mary Ann Ronconi

New Amsterdam Home
Senior Living At Its Finest
June 8, 1999

My dear Rika,

It was nice of you to write to a very distant and very old cousin. I am a week away from my 105th birthday. There is a good nurse here who does anything I ask to keep me going. I haven't been able to write since I was 102, so she has found me a recorder. Now I can tell you stories of our branch of the family for your book since it is long past the time when the New York Van Arsdales were such important people in the city.

Our descent can be blamed on me. I was the only son and heir to the family business. But I just never had any taste for it. It caused an awful row that evening in May of 1914.

The butler had just announced the dinner menu as he did every evening as soon as we sat down at table. I was very nervous knowing I had to tell them that I would not use the degree I had just earned at Columbia College to come work for Father and add a fifth generation to the plaque outside our doors on Park Avenue. When I said I intended to go on to medical school, Father's ire rose to majestic heights. He shouted and raged until the crystal goblets next to our Limoges plates bounced and came close to chipping them. Such waves formed in the finger bowls that water splashed onto the starched linen tablecloth.

"A sawbones," he sniggered finally. "You will spend your career maiming people when you could be presenting them at their handsomest, looking as good as they ever have in their lives." I argued that he was still living in the Civil War. Medicine had made great strides. Surgeons did not just cut off limbs. They delivered children from the agony of endless sore throats taking out infected tonsils. They saved lives removing rupturing appendixes and festering gallbladders. When I got to what I would do for those body parts at the end of the digestive track, Mother picked up the servants' bell and rang it frantically for the next course, abruptly ending the battle.

We reached a compromise, my father and I. He would not pay the tuition. I would earn it working for him as I attended medical school. There is no doubt in my mind that he expected I would flag or flunk out, but in the end the work gave me a leg up over most of my fellow students. As we did many jobs side by side, he shared the history and some dark secrets of the Van Arsdales with me.

I graduated with honors but never practiced in the City. After service in the Great War, I stayed in the army and served on bases all over the country. I never found a wife. He lost all hope that I would succeed him or produce another generation of Van Arsdales. When Father's gout made standing and walking too painful, he sold the business and retired with my mother to Savannah.

Thus ended, my dear Rika, the Van Arsdales' long and glorious history as morticians. In the trade we were known as embalmers to the presidents. My grandfather Harmanus traveled all the way to Kinderhook in 1862 for Martin Van Buren. Chester A. Arthur was more considerate since

Harmanus was getting on in age. He died right here in New York City in 1886 but required special attention, as reflected in the Van Arsdale Mortuary ledger, because he had to make it all the way to Albany for burial.

We were among the very first to practice the mortician's art in New York, rising above the common undertaker who was not much more that an iceman and a gravedigger. But even he was an advance over the tradition of the women of the family laying out the dead. The new aspiring middle class washed and dressed their dear departed, then called in the undertaker. He arrived with a man-sized zinc tub and a large cake of ice which he set up in the front parlor. He covered that with waterproof canvas and topped it all off with a black velvet covering. The wake lasted as long as the ice. With ice cut from Upstate lakes shipped down the Hudson and preserved in sawdust, a wake could go on for several days, even in the summer, allowing relatives to come from far and wide to view their revered uncle or brother or mother or grandmother before burial – and be present for the reading of the will.

But a cake of ice will not do for defunct dignitaries of private or public means. Mayors, bishops, bankers, generals and presidents expect to lie in state for as much as a week or even two if they have attracted sufficient adulation – or loathing – during their time above the ground. (It was my father's firm opinion, born of experience, that loathing draws more *viewers* – hardly could he call them mourners – than love or esteem.) So, while a family could get by in the undertaking business, to get rich one had to become a mortician, a practitioner of the art of embalming in a laboratory-like setting, the mortuary. This was an art newly revived in Europe in the days when the Van Arsdales had had enough of just getting by as undertakers. Grandfather Harmanus Van Arsdale made the family's first return to Holland since 1638 to learn the chemistry and the art of human pickling.

Such was his success as a student and then a practitioner that the Van Arsdale Mortuary left the lowly undertakers of New York on the ice, so to speak. Harmanus was the mortician of choice of the finest or, at least, the best-known and well-heeled New Yorkers when the man Lincoln appointed to save the Union on the battlefield, General U.S. Grant, put down his last glass. His two terms as president had taken the shine off his reputation and the American public had let him drift into alcoholic oblivion and penury. When he knew his days were numbered he somehow put off the grim reaper - and put down the whiskey bottle - long enough to write his memoirs. They were his hope that at least posthumously he could ensure the financial improvement of his impoverished family. Hardly had the ink dried before he died on July 23, 1885.

It was a virtual pack of beggars, therefore, who came to Grandpa Harmanus offering him the honor of laying their father in state. With an eye to ingratiating his services with several gilded families whose wealth had oozed from Grant's second term and after a whiff of the mortal remains, Harmanus magnanimously accepted the unprofitable honor of laying out the impecunious ex-president. Grant would be Harmanus' third president and my father's first.

While not profitable neither was it costly. For once no travel was involved. The funeral *and* the grave would be in New York City. The years of drinking nothing less than 100 proof rye ensured that U.S. could withstand at least 10 more days in this world without the injection of expensive preservatives. The general and president with just some cheap cosmetics was presentably pickled, and the Van Arsdale Mortuary was not out a cent when he was lowered into the grave on August 8, 1885.

But no good deed goes unpunished. Grant's last minute memoirs came back to haunt Harmanus and my father, almost undoing the reputation of the Van Arsdale Mortuary. The memoirs were enormously successful in that sentimental age and a collection plate went round the nation to build a memorial to U.S. Grant. The plate came back full and construction began on what became, upon completion in 1897, the largest mausoleum in the country. As construction progressed Harmanus became more and more alarmed. My father swore that his father's hair turned white overnight in 1895 when he realized that in only two years U.S. Grant would be resurrected from the grave. His coffin would surely be opened with the expectation that a Van Arsdale-embalmed president would emerge perfectly preserved and ready for a second going. But they had done a ten-day job not a ten-year one. General Grant was not going to pass inspection as he moved into his new and glorious digs.

It was my father, Schuyler Van Arsdale, who saved the day in the dead of night in 1895. I was but a babe of one at the time. With two years for the grass to grow over the disturbed plots, Father got hold of a pair of illiterate barflies who would occasionally wield shovels at odd hours for pay. He employed them to dig up two graves, the pickled ex-president's and that of an exquisitely Van Arsdale-embalmed Chinaman of great wealth and scholarship. Much venerated as a spirit by his family, the Van Arsdales knew for certain his Chinese relatives would never, ever, request to see his splendid mortal remains again. Such a sight could deal a death blow of fright. Grant, in truly bad repair, went into the much finer casket of the Chinaman and back into the ground upon the spot. The Chinaman, transferred to the modest coffin that the penniless Grants had chosen ten years before, was transported to the mortuary.

Now a great mortician is also an accomplished make-up artist. Chinamen just do not have the full and luxuriant beard that makes Grant so fine looking in Matthew Brady's battlefield photographs. But when young Schuy and old Harmanus finished up their make-over, the man headed for Grant's Tomb had such a beard that it all but obscured the eyes above it. They were ready to assert ("Gentlemen, it is common knowledge") that hair continues to grow after death. The diggers, having taken their payment directly to the nearest saloon, were out of commission when the new U.S. Grant was ready to go back into the ground leaving my forebears no choice but to take care of the re-interment themselves – a task they had always considered, no pun intended, beneath them. Leaning heavily upon his shovel over the just re-filled grave, Harmanus clutched his heart and gasped to his exhausted son, "Schuyler, the man was a Chinese scholar. We neglected to do a manicure. We must dig him back up."

"Father, no!" Schuy exclaimed, gulping for air as much from dread as exertion. But the family genius, I am proud to say, came to life in my father's mind as he moved shakily to pick up his shovel once more. "Father, think again! We do not have to dig another shovelful. Everyone believes fingernails are like hair. They too grow after death."

As no one wanted to insult the great general's family when the monumental tomb was completed above the Hudson River in New York City, the coffin that came out of the ground for the second and last time was deemed acceptable. After all, the dignitaries charged with the move concurred, it would be encased in a magnificent sarcophagus; no need to spend money on a fine new casket no one will see. Not much different from the Chinaman's family, the Grant children expressed no desire to view their father's mortal remains after ten years in the ground. The coffin was never re-opened, so the six-inch nails on the hands of the scholarly occupant of Grant's Tomb, a certain Mr. Hu, never contributed to the myth of nails – like hair - continuing to grow after death.

There you have it, dear cousin. The real truth. For decades it has been a silly joke to pull on the ignorant, asking who is buried in Grant's Tomb. Groucho Marx made a habit of it back in the early days of television. I wanted to go on his show and tell him he wasn't so smart at all. *The question is the answer: Who is buried in Grant's Tomb? Hu is buried in Grant's Tomb. Not Grant. Hu!*

So sorry. I didn't mean to raise my voice. Nurse Herrington will come running and say that is enough for now. She is very nervous I won't make it to 105. She must have a large bet on me. I tell her she shouldn't worry because I have yet to find the work of the morticians hereabouts up to Van Arsdale standards-and believe me, my fellow residents here at the New Amsterdam Home provide plenty of examples. So until I find one who can do a job of such quality on yours truly, I am not going anywhere.

Looking forward to reading your book, I am your fifth cousin twice removed,

    Cornelis Van Arsdale ■

The Waif and The Void

by

Lana Bella

a lonely waif's agony
fills the autumnal mooring
tethering the muddy embankment
of the still graveyard,
you can hear it through the sounds
of the oiled pelicans and
returned waves,

your spilled fingers
from inside the jacket's holes
reach out toward her orbit,
you, a dash between the rock salt
and her intricate bones,
know the surest shelter is
somewhere among the birds and
the void,

what propelled her down
to this dark-hewn dune you'll never
know, but you mute your light
into the westerly wind as it carries
her ripples sideways to
where the sand grows damp
from her tears,

moving away from yourself
without knowing, you tilt into the axis
of her songs, your mind fingers
the puzzle that still pivots
in silence, toying to the thought

Witch

by

Kate Wiant

And she sits at the grave with a stitch in her side,
An old woman with an old-raw-hide
Hung for blasphemy, hung for money
Hung for land, for greed, oh honey.

And she waits with the patience of saints
For sinners who feign would pray, would faint
Whose false idols hung about wrist, hung on neck,
Hung in fat pocket books, hung on walls, for prospect.

And modestly they come, and she follows them home.
An old specter with sickness to spread.
Hung on sheets, hung on bed
Hung on little, innocent head, oh honey.

Made in the USA
Lexington, KY
20 August 2016